Back Roads of Membertou County

a novel

Alfred Silver

Pottersfield Press, Lawrencetown Beach, Nova Scotia, Canada

Copyright © 2006 Alfred Silver

All rights reserved. No part of this publication may be reproduced or used or transmitted in any form or by any means – graphic, electronic or mechanical, including photocopying – or by any information storage or retrieval system, without the prior, written permission of the publisher. Any requests for photocopying, recording, taping or information storage and retrieval systems of any part of this book shall be directed in writing to Access Copyright, The Canadian Copyright Licensing Agency, 1 Yonge Street, Suite 1900, Toronto, Ontario M5E 1E5. This also applies to classroom use.

Library and Archives Canada Cataloguing in Publication

Silver, Alfred, 1951-

Back roads of Membertou County : a novel / Alfred Silver.

ISBN 1-895900-81-6

I. Title.

PS8587.I27B33 2006   C813'.54   903762-0

Front cover photo: istockphoto

Cover design: Gail Leblanc

Pottersfield Press acknowledges the ongoing support of The Canada Council for the Arts, as well as the Nova Scotia Department of Tourism, Culture and Heritage, Cultural Affairs Division. We also acknowledge the financial support of the Government of Canada through the Book Publishing Industry Development Program for our publishing activities.

Pottersfield Press
83 Leslie Road
East Lawrencetown
Nova Scotia, Canada, B2Z 1P8
Website: www.pottersfieldpress.com
To order, phone 1-800-NIMBUS9 (1-800-646-2879)
Printed in Canada

1

Corporal Kowalchuck picked up his standard-issue, long-barrelled RCMP flashlight before stepping out of his patrol car. He switched it on when the dome light went out, as the door thunked shut behind him. The crunch of gravel under his boots lasted only a couple of steps before he was off the driveway and onto the lawn. "Yard," he corrected himself. By and large, people in Membertou County, Nova Scotia, didn't care if what grew around their houses was certified lawn grass or cooch-grass and dandelions, as long as it was green and could be mowed.

Corporal Kowalchuck stopped and stood shining his flashlight around. What the beam showed him was fairly typical of a rural, Maritimes backyard, if the people who lived there had more time than money and spent a lot of that time outside. There were staked and wired rows of what might be blackberries or raspberries, some tall bushes that might be lilacs – hard to tell with only the buds of leaves yet showing – stone-bordered flowerbeds, a huge, old pine tree with a tire swing hanging from a bough.

Even though he'd arrived with his siren on and rooflights flashing, no one came out to ask Corporal Kowalchuck what he was doing, or tell him what they were doing. It didn't surprise him. In some ways, being a police officer was like being an outlaw: outside the community, with people always suspicious of your motives.

Corporal Kowalchuck moved farther into the yard, and his flashlight beam found what it was searching for. A human body was lying face-down in the grass, the blood around it mixing with the dew. Corporal Kowalchuck didn't have to look closer to know who it was, or that it was a definitely dead body. His job was just to not disturb anything, and secure the area until the homicide and forensics investigators arrived.

As Corporal Kowalchuck unspooled the yellow Crime Scene tape from tree to tree, he tried to unspool the chain of accidents that had somehow led to a non-accidental firearms fatality in the backyard of a tidy little bungalow on the edge of a quiet little village. He supposed it had started about nine months ago, which seemed a perverse reversal of what nine months traditionally led to. In fact, now that he thought about it, he could trace the exact minute when it started, because he'd looked at his watch . . .

* * *

Corporal Kowalchuck twisted his left wrist just enough to be able to see the luminous hands on his watch without moving his hands out of the proper ten to two position on the steering wheel. The watch read more like two to ten. He supposed he should probably join the twenty-first century and get himself a digital watch with LED. It'd be some decades yet before he'd have the excuse of being an old fogy. But digital watches didn't give you any context.

What mattered at the moment was he had an appointment at 10 p.m. and he was ten kilometres from where he should be, and heading in the opposite direction. The next exit where he could turn around was a good twenty kilometres away, but just ahead was an access road across the ditch between the eastbound and westbound sides of the highway. The access road was for Authorized Vehicles Only, but if the vehicle of the Detachment Commander of the Raddallton Area RCMP Rural & Highways Division wasn't authorized, whose was?

Kowalchuck shifted into the left-hand lane and slowed down,

switching on the roof lights for the benefit of anyone zooming up behind him who wasn't brake light literate. When he reached the narrow gravel access road, he turned onto it carefully. They would love it in the Raddallton bars if a Mountie had to call a tow truck because one of his wheels missed the road in the dark. When the nose of the patrol car reached the edge of the hardtop, Kowalchuck stopped and peered to his right for any ghost of headlights poking over the ridge. The majority of the names on the Honour Roll of RCMP officers killed on duty were of highway fatalities.

Once the patrol car was pointed in the right direction, Kowalchuck hit the siren and booted it. When he pulled into the parking lot behind the detachment, there was a vehicle he'd never seen there before: a mid-sized car neither old nor new, of a nondescript colour. Nondescript seemed to be the order of business. The Federal Excise Agent had requested a night meeting to minimize the chances that some passerby might notice him and blow his cover. Kowalchuck hadn't even spoken to the agent on the phone; the meeting had been arranged long-distance from an office in Ottawa.

Corporal Kowalchuck quick-marched into the detachment and towards his office. En route, he glanced at Marni behind the glass in the dispatcher's booth. She raised her eyebrows and pointed toward the closed door of his office. He nodded that he'd expected someone to be waiting for him there. She lowered her hand and one eyebrow, but kept the other eyebrow raised, and quirked up that corner of her mouth. Odd. Kowalchuck brushed it off and kept on going.

Corporal Kowalchuck opened the door of his office saying, "Sorry I'm late, but I . . ." then trailed off. Seated cross-legged on the chair in front of his desk was a woman a few years older than him, maybe thirty-five, with expensively short-cut, semi-blonde hair, and black eyebrows. On his desk was some sort of slumbering, cat-sized creature, with curly black hair. Kowalchuck realized the creature was a wig, and turned his eyes from it back to the woman. She was wearing not-new jeans that looked spraypainted on, and a shrinkwrap, scoop-necked, purple, stretch T-shirt. That was actually a fairly blend-in costume around Membertou County. Country girls tended to favour skin-tight, low-necked clothing, sometimes when they were past the age and conditioning when country boys would want to see them in clinging clothing. This one definitely wasn't.

The woman didn't seem miffed at Kowalchuck's surprise, maybe even a little pleased. She said, "Federal Excise Agents come in all shapes and sizes, Corporal. And there's no need to apologize for being a little late. I did my time in patrol cars before this. Things come up, unexpectedly."

Kowalchuck unbuckled his heavy ordnance belt and stripped it off, saying, "Can I get you anything? Coffee? Oh." He noticed the cup on the corner of the desk nearest to her.

"Your dispatcher already got me one. Not bad for stationhouse coffee. If you want to get one for yourself, I don't mind waiting."

"No, thanks. One more and I'll start vibrating." He sat in his desk chair, opened the bottom drawer and took out the half-emptied bottle of Gatorade. "Well, what can I do for you?" Since she hadn't introduced herself, he figured her name wasn't going to figure in the etiquette of the conversation.

"We've been operating in Northwest Membertou County for the last little while, and are about to expand operations south into your district. Some local residents whose names came up in our investigations may be familiar to you, or not."

"Shoot."

She took a notebook out of her purse and opened it. "Margaret McLean."

"That's a fairly common name around here."

"Resident of New Oak Township."

"Oh. A couple of prior convictions for drug possession, I believe, and something to do with a stolen car. There were rumours she was involved with a growhouse operation, but nothing substantable. I could pull the file."

"No need. Not yet. This is just preliminary." The excise

agent jotted something in her notebook and went on with her list. Some of the names rang no bells with Corporal Kowalchuck, some had pending or prior charges of things like trafficking drugs, bootlegging, living off the avails of prostitution, some had only rumours attached to them. And then: "Ben Marsden."

Kowalchuck leaned his chair back and cocked his head, and he could feel his eyebrows crinkling together. "Ben Marsden?"

"Yes. Sometimes known as Big Ben Marsden. Of Piziquid Village. You know him?"

"A little. I know his wife better."

The excise agent smirked, in a friendly kind of way.

"Uh, maybe I could've phrased that better. Mrs. Marsden was very helpful to us in an investigation last year. Provided me with some important information I might not've discovered otherwise."

"Hm. Seems husband and wife are working opposite sides of the fence."

"What do you mean?" He knew that Ben Marsden probably rounded off a few corners here and there, but nothing in the line of major criminal activity.

The excise agent shook her head, in the universal police shorthand of 'ongoing investigation.' "We're only collecting information at this time. What information do you have of Mr. and Mrs. Marsden?"

"Well, they're both in their mid- to late-forties, I'd say. Mr. Marsden lost his steady employment some years ago, not unusual around here, and has been doing odd jobs to get by. Mrs. Marsden was loans officer at the local credit union until fairly recently, when they found an excuse to dump her for a younger person at an entry-level salary."

The excise officer clucked her tongue and shook her head in disgust at that kind of behaviour.

"Since then, Mrs. Marsden has been working as a cleaning lady, cleaning other people's houses."

"Smart."

That came from so far out of nowhere that it threw Kowalchuck back into a prairies phrase he'd been trying to cure himself of, since east coast people didn't seem to know what to do with it. "How's that?"

"Oh, just speculation at this point." The excise agent went back to her list. After a few more minutes, she closed her notebook and said, "That's all she wrote. Thank you for being so cooperative with me, Corporal."

"That's what I'm here for."

The excise agent put her notebook away, then propped her left elbow on the arm of her chair and lowered her head enough to put the tip of her left forefinger between her lips to press against her front teeth. She held that position for a moment, slightly nodding her head in a rhythm that seemed timed to her pulse. Then she lowered her hand and raised her head, looked at him across the desk and said, "But, you know, sometimes there are bits of information that don't come to mind in a formal, police-business setting. My billet is only about forty-five minutes from here, but across the district line, where you wouldn't be recognized out of uniform. When you get off duty you could meet me there, and we could see if anything else comes to mind . . . in a more informal setting."

Corporal Kowalchuck didn't quite know what to respond. It was no news flash that people who were on the road could get up to behaviour they wouldn't at home, and that certainly included the off-hours of an undercover agent on a weeks-long operation. And undercover agents couldn't get much in the way of intimate socializing without blowing their cover. Then again, maybe this pink-frosted-lipped, smoky-eyed excise agent was just being business-like, and had meant only and exactly what she'd said.

Kowalchuck decided it was better to make a fool of himself and respond as though the very attractive woman across the desk from him had been suggesting more than police business. Then again, there might be a way to say it that would fit both possibilities. He said, "Thank you, but, uh, I'm sorry, I'm pre-engaged."

"Lucky girl."

"Well, um . . . not necessarily."

* * *

Bonnie Marsden stood behind her surprise-child's chair, trying to brush the last tangles out of Melissa's silky, honey-blonde hair without interfering with her breakfast. Twelve years after Robbie, and eleven years after Bonnie had gone through the operation to have her tubes tied, along came Melissa. The surprise had turned out to be a blessing, most days, and at the moment the particular blessing was that Melissa's hair had stayed baby-straight, instead of curling up tight and troublesome like her mother's. And it seemed likely that Melissa's hair would either stay honey-blonde or go coppery-hazel like her father's, instead of the mud-brown that had made her mother spend more money on dye jobs than office clothes.

Two weeks of grade primary, what the old folks called Kindergarten, had got both mother and daughter almost used to the routine. Bonnie almost wished they hadn't had to get used to it so soon. Back in Bonnie's day, grade primary hadn't been mandatory, so she'd been allowed another year of being a footloose kid without Structured Instructional Activity. Of course, in most families in those days, both parents didn't have to have jobs. And at least Melissa had squeaked by before they made pre-primary mandatory. Bonnie wasn't quite sure what she thought of having children mostly raised by expert agents of the state. That had worked out great in Russia.

The back door banged open and Bonnie turned to see her bear-sized, russet-haired husband at the foot of the little staircase, wiping rain off his forehead. He kicked off his boots and padded up the stairs, saying, "I got Clyde hutched up to his line no problem, he's getting used to the routine."

"Lotta that going on around here."

"I just hope he's got the sense to go into his doghouse. Sometimes in a pelting rain, old Floyd'd just sit out in the open and . . ." Ben trailed off as Bonnie flicked him a glance. It wasn't good for Melissa to be reminded of old Floyd, who never got to be "old" Floyd. For that matter, it'd be a while yet before Bonnie didn't get a tight throat thinking of Floyd and the way he died. "Clyde was barking like a maniac at that helicopter, trying to scare it off."

"Helicopter? I didn't hear, I've had the radio up to hear the weather."

Ben sat down in front of his coffee cup, took a sip, made a face and got up to pour in some hot from the pot. He said, "Well, I don't need the radio to tell me it's raining medium-hard now, and gonna be pis – *pelt*ing down pretty soon." He cocked an eyebrow in Melissa's direction, and it seemed he'd deked his way out of putting another quarter in the swear jar.

Bonnie patted the top of Melissa's cereal-crunching head and said, "Sounds like you get a ride down to the schoolbus, honey, instead of walking."

Ben murmured, "Funny about that helicopter. I only saw it for a second, but kept hearing it. Sounded like it was over our woodlot, flying low and slow, and not really going anywhere, just sorta back and forth. Maybe looking for somebody lost in the woods . . . ?"

"The radio didn't say anything about somebody lost in the woods."

Ben chuckled. "Maybe the *pilot*'s lost."

Bonnie went over to the three municipality-mandated plastic bins against the wall, to clean off the brush. She hesitated for a second, then decided that hair wasn't recyclable or compostable and opened the garbage bin. She said, "After I get Melissa on the bus I'll just keep on going to clean Bela's place."

Ben interrupted his coffee cup on its way to his mouth. "*Bela's?*"

"Oh, sorry." Bonnie laughed at herself. She'd long had a habit of identifying people and situations by old movies. Her first two kids had been colicky, so she'd put in a lot of time watching the Late Movie, or Late Late Late Movie, from her yard sale rocking chair with a slumbering infant in her arms, knowing that the instant she stopped rocking, baby Moyle or baby Darcy was going to start squalling again. The screen images had stuck in her mind, and made for a convenient personal shorthand. But sometimes she forgot that other people weren't in on the joke. "That old Hungarian guy who bought a little house on the edge of Raddallton to be near his grandkids. The way he talks reminds me of Bela Lugosi. What've you got on today?"

"Well, I don't need a phone call to tell me that roof job won't be on today. So . . . seems to me I promised Miss Melissa I'd clean up and paint that old desk you got for her at the yard sale." He turned to Melissa. "Whadaya think of that, pumpkin?"

Melissa nodded enthusiastically and "*Mmm*"ed around her mouthful of blackberry and cereal.

Ben turned back to Bonnie. "I figure I'll take a pot of tea out to the barn, maybe a little something to flavour it, and potter away at the desk and a few other bits and pieces, have myself a quiet little rainy day."

"Sounds like a nice kind of day."

"Sounds like a real nice day."

* * *

An hour or so later, Ben was sitting on a lawn chair on the dry side of the open barn door, watching the rain roar down and pondering colour schemes. The "barn" was actually a barn-shaped double garage, and they actually didn't even park their vehicles in it, except when Ben was grafting on a bit of sheet metal to pass the annual safety inspection. Mostly the barn housed Ben's tools and workbench, and the stacks, boxes and jars of odds and ends he'd brought home from jobsites and other places. So far Ben had managed to clean the cobwebs and dust off the desk with industrial-strength TSP – or PTS, as it said on the French side of the box, damned confusing – and rough-sanded it enough that the remaining old varnish would take enamel. The question was, which of the tail-ends of paint cans would go together? He'd just about decided on lime green for the body and pink for the drawers, when Clyde started barking like a maniac and didn't stop.

There was no sound of a loud truck or boombox car trespassing on Clyde's road, so Ben stepped out into the rain to have a look. Clyde was straining at the far end of his line, looking like somebody'd just emptied a lake on him. He had a perfectly good doghouse, but it seemed he was going to do like Floyd and not go in there except in the worst of blizzards. Maybe the both of them had got it from doing time in a cage in the pound, a terror of being trapped again. Well, like Floyd, Clyde was half waterdog anyway, son of that mythical, seminal black lab that seemed to've visited every long-haired female in Membertou County.

Ben looked in the direction Clyde's nose and barks were pointed. Hiking out of the woods at the bottom of the yard were two people who weren't dressed for this weather; anything short of a sou'wester, slicker and hip boots wasn't dressed-for-this-weather. Ben didn't much like strangers coming onto his property, but at least he could give them the chance to explain themselves or clear off. He called out, "Hello!" partly to get their attention, and partly to let them know there was someone at home, and a large someone at that.

They didn't turn and run back into the woods, but Ben could see them hesitate, sensibly leery of the medium-sized black dog with large-sized white teeth. Ben called, "He's a pound dog, he won't quit! So just circle around the end of his line. That's the kind of cable they use to hold down airplanes, so it'll prob'ly hold. Take it easy, Clyde."

Clyde didn't take it much easier. As the two strangers circled around to the gravel driveway and approached the barn, Ben could see they were a man and a woman, both thirty-something, both with their hair rain-plastered to their heads, and their Gore-Tex jackets drenched past the saturation point. The man said, "Hi, I'm Jim Taylor, and this is my wife, Amy."

The wife said, "Hi."

"Ben Marsden."

"We were wondering of you might be able to do us a favour? We'd pay you for it."

That sounded interesting; no one else was offering to pay Ben to do anything today. He said, "First off, you could do *me* a favour and step in before I get as soaked through as you two."

In the barn, Ben reached down two folded lawn chairs and handed them over, saying, "I better get some heat on before you two drowned rats catch pneumonia. Snug your chairs in close." He opened the grate of the old potbelly stove whose flue pipe wasn't exactly up to code, and crumpled in some newspaper with a bit of kindling on top. The paper was humidified and took a moment to catch, but soon it was crackling enough for Ben to put in a couple of sticks of firewood and close the grate. While Ben was doing that, the male drowned rat said, "This is kind of embarrassing to admit, the fix I got us into, but . . . We were scouting out camping spots for our vacation next week, September's the best month for camping –"

Amy Taylor put in, "Still warm, but no flies or mosquitoes." Ben just grunted and nodded that was true.

"But," Jim Taylor went on, "I overestimated the traction of my little sports truck. We got stuck in the mud on an old logging road back there –"

"Were you the helicopter?"

"Helicopter?"

"Yeah, there was a helicopter around this morning, circling back and forth like it was looking for somebody lost in the woods."

Jim Taylor seemed confused about what to say to that, but his wife jumped in with, "No, we only got stuck about twenty minutes ago, so if they were looking for somebody, it wasn't us. We could see the roofs of houses down the hill, so we figured our best bet was to hike down here and find a road that'd maybe lead us to a gas station with a tow truck. And then, we came out into your yard and saw that big old four-wheel drive pickup."

Ben said, "Some days it's a four-wheel drive. Some days you have to start it with a hammer." He stood up from the stove and shook the teapot. "There's still enough in here to get a start at warming you up, and I'll put the kettle on."

As Ben was reaching down two of the spare cups he kept handy in the barn, Jim Taylor said, "Uh, Ben, I don't mean to sound ungrateful, but you wouldn't happen to have anything stronger than tea? Amy's shivering pretty bad . . ."

Ben thought about it and looked the two Taylors over again. They both were definitely soaked through and their sneakers were covered in cold mud, as were the hems of their jeans and one knee where one of them had taken a fall. The woman had a scratch on the side of her face from some kind of bramble, and she truly was shivering: her voice had quavered when she spoke, and she didn't seem the tremulous type. Ben went to his workbench and moved a few of the jars of nails forward from the wall, saying, "Well, I do have a pint bottle of springwater, or at least part of a pint . . ."

"Uh, springwater isn't exactly what I was thinking of . . ."

"Oh, this is Membertou County springwater, about a hundred-and-forty proof." Ben reached down into the space behind that section of the workbench and came out with a plastic mickey bottle that still had most of a white rum label on it. He poured a little into the two guest cups, and added a dollop to the remnants of his tea.

Jim Taylor sipped and exhaled. "Man, that's good stuff! You ever had moonshine before, Amy?"

"No, but it sure does the trick."

"I haven't had a drink of shine for years, and it sure wasn't as smooth as this. Can I buy a bottle off you, Ben? I'd pay top dollar."

"It's not for sale." Ben didn't go into the details of what the old girl he got it from had told him, what her grandfather had dinned into her head as the first commandment of moonshining: never, never, never, never sell. Moonshine was for home and friends, or trading for sides of beef or yard work. The minute some greedy idiot started selling, the heat came down on everybody.

A disembodied, crackly voice suddenly snapped into the barn. Both Taylors jumped in their chairs, Jim so much that he spilled a few drops. Ben took the pager off his belt to show them it was nothing spooky. "Volunteer Fire Department. Just the daily test. You two are kind of nervous."

Amy Taylor said, with a bit of a laugh and no more quaver in her voice, "Well, what with the truck getting stuck in the middle of nowhere, and then scrambling through the woods in a monsoon, I guess every little surprise seems like it's going to bring another disaster."

"I guess it would."

They sat for awhile, sipping and chatting. The steam stopped coming off the drowned rats' clothes, but Jim Taylor didn't stop angling back to different tacks at trying to get Ben to sell him some Membertou County springwater. The fifth or sixth tack was: "I sure would like to give a taste of this to your cousin from Cape Breton, Amy – whatsisname?"

"Ian."

"Always bragging about the stuff they make back in the hills up there. I'd sure like to give him a show-up of what real shine tastes like."

Ben said exasperatedly, "Oh hell, *take* it, there's hardly any left in the bottle anyway. We better go get your truck pulled out of the mud while we still can. But once we do, you better let Amy do the driving, Jim. I never seen anybody for putting back the shine like you."

Jim laughed happily. "Gotta get it while you can, Ben."

* * *

A few days later, Bonnie was sitting down to lunch when Ben came home. Or dinner, as the neighbours would put it. The country habit was breakfast, dinner, supper, instead of the city's breakfast, lunch, dinner. It was getting jumbled together as more city people bought places in the country to commute from and more country kids got into city habits through university or jobs. Sometimes it was guesswork whether somebody'd just said they would drop by the house after the noon meal or in the evening.

But the only confusion about this midday meal was, as Bonnie said when Ben came through the door, "I thought you'd be working on that roof all day."

"So did I. But the contractor got hisself double-booked, 'cause of the rainstorm, so he put on a double crew to get it all done and capped and crowned by noontime. He'll pay me for the whole day anyway."

"He will?"

Ben glanced at her with what she thought of as his long-distance look, from a place whose area code she didn't know and had no intentions of looking up. After all these years, there was still a place or two inside him that she didn't quite get, and she thought it was probably better that way. Ben said flatly, "He will."

Ben sat down across from her and opened the Daffy Duck lunchbox that had been Robbie's until Robbie grew too sophisticated, back around grade seven seven years ago. The phone rang. Bonnie was closer to the phone and Ben had his mouth full, so she picked it up. "Hello?"

"Mrs. Marsden, it's Corporal Kowalchuck. Might I speak with your husband, please?"

"Uh, sure. Just a sec. Ben, it's for you, it's Corporal Kowalchuck."

"Huh? Hope there hasn't been an accident." Ben took the phone, and she could only hear his side of the conversation. "Yeah? Well, yeah, I guess I could. But, why? Yeah, okay."

Ben hung up the phone, looking extremely puzzled. He muttered, "Weird."

"What?"

"Uh, he asked me if I could get myself down to the Mountie station by a half-hour or so."

"Why?"

"Well, I asked him that. He said he couldn't tell me till I got down there. And he said something else. He said it'd be better for me if I went in voluntarily, 'stead of them coming to get me."

2

Ben parked his truck in front of the wide, low Mountie building and headed in, wondering what in hell they were calling him in for. It couldn't be the several straight-cash jobs he'd done last year. That'd be a letter from the tax department, and there was no way the government could've found out about those anyway. It couldn't've been the safety sticker he'd bought for twice the government price, because it would've cost him five times that for an up-to-code job on the body work he'd faked with tin and tar. It couldn't be the frozen chickens and other food items that'd fallen off the backs of trucks; the evidence had long been eaten. Anyway, his purchases of items of mysterious origin had been cut back since Bonnie stopped being predictably away from home during business hours.

The receptionist said, "Hi," as though she knew him, and pressed a button on her console. Maybe somebody's niece he'd last seen when she was twelve years old.

Corporal Kowalchuck came out of his office, opened the wicket gate and said, "Please come this way, Mr. Marsden." Ben accompanied him down a hallway to a door that Kowalchuck opened and then stepped aside from, gesturing Ben to go in first. *Right,* Ben nodded to himself, *you never let the suspect get behind you.*

Beyond the doorway were no surprises. Ben had been in

those kind of rooms before, though not for a long time, and they were all pretty much the same: greenish-yellowish enamelled cinder block walls, a metal desk with rounded corners, and two or three sturdy metal chairs. This room was only different than the others in that it had a side door. The door was undoubtedly steel under the brown enamel, and undoubtedly locked.

In most business offices, the visitor would sit in front of the desk. But Ben knew the other rule: *Never let the suspect get between you and the door.* Ben went and sat behind the desk. Kowalchuck stayed standing and said, "It's good of you to come in on such short notice, Mr. Marsden."

"Didn't seem like I had much choice."

"Well, we can save a lot of preliminaries if I just introduce you to a couple of people." Kowalchuck opened the side door – so much for 'undoubtedly locked' – and said to someone beyond it, "Would you step in here for a moment, please."

What came through the doorway was a pair of people fresh in Ben's memory, although they weren't dripping wet and shivering now. Ben looked from the male half of the couple to the female and back again. Kowalchuck said, "The two people you know as Jim and Amy Taylor, Mr. Marsden, are agents of the Federal Excise Department."

Ben's hands opened and closed several times. He muttered, "Cute. Real friggin' cute."

The male agent said jauntily, "*We* thought so."

The female agent said, "We'll be in the next room, Corporal, if you need us for anything."

Kowalchuck closed the door behind them, sat down in front of the desk and opened a manilla folder. "You are being charged, Mr. Marsden, with trafficking in illegal, contraband liquor."

"I don't know anything about illegal contra-whatsit. Us hillbillies just call it moonshine."

"Whatever you want to call it, the agents report that you sold them a pint bottle of –"

"I never sold them anything!"

"The agents testify they paid you twenty dollars."

"That was for pulling their goddamn truck out of the mud!"

It seemed to Ben that Kowalchuck's lean face suddenly got a bit of a flush in it. It was hard to tell with Kowalchuck, since he was naturally darkish, almost Indian-looking. But it did seem to Ben that a trace of pink appeared along his cheekbones. Kowalchuck stood up and said, "Would you wait here a moment, please, Mr. Marsden."

"It don't look like I'm going anywhere."

* * *

Corporal Kowalchuck closed the door to the side room behind him and looked to the two excise agents. They were sitting on opposite sides of a desk, leafing through a stack of folders. Kowalchuck said, trying to keep his voice level, "Mr. Marsden informs me that that twenty dollars was for 'pulling your goddamn truck out of the mud.'"

The woman said, "If you read our report carefully, Corporal, you'll see we both corroborate that, during the course of the operation, Mr. Marsden received twenty dollars from us, and we received from him a pint bottle of illegal, contraband liquor."

Kowalchuck had to breathe through his teeth a few times before he could say relatively evenly, "So a magistrate might logically assume . . ." They both looked blandly back at him. "If you pull any more of that sleazy shit in my jurisdiction, I'll include in my report that you tried to inflate the charges."

"This investigation is a lot bigger than Membertou County, Corporal. Your job is to assist us in any way you can."

"My job is to enforce the *law*. Which isn't made any easier by other enforcement agents playing cute tricks with the law to feed their ambitions. I will proceed with the interrogation as per recommendations."

* * *

Ben was watching those concrete walls close in on him, when

Kowalchuck came back into the room, sat down and said, "You are being charged, Mr. Marsden, with *possession* of illegal contraband liquor. Would you like to have a lawyer present before I proceed with the interview? If you are unable to afford a lawyer, I can contact Legal Aid."

"Don't seem to be much point, seems pretty cut and dried."

"Very well. There is a good chance the charge will be dropped, if you inform us where you got the . . . moonshine."

"Sure. Old Morley Bishop."

Kowalchuck started noting in his notebook and said, "Do you know where I might find Mr. Bishop?"

"'Might' ain't in it. You can always find him in the same place. Southwest corner, Piziquid Village cemetery. Went for a drive with somebody who'd drunk more of his stuff than he had."

Kowalchuck stopped writing. "How long has he been there?"

"About a year and a half, just before your time."

"Are you expecting me to believe you had that pint sitting in your barn for a year and a half?"

"Well, it don't go bad. Long as you leave the cap on."

Kowalchuck put down his pen and notebook. "I think you should start taking this a lot more seriously, Ben. This isn't just a police matter. Federal Excise Agents have a lot more powers than standard-issue police officers."

"Powers like what?"

"For one thing, they can impound your vehicle, since it was used to transport illegal contraband liquor."

Ben leaned his chair back, propped one boot on the corner of the desk to slacken the angle of his right hip, delved into his right-hand jeans pocket for the truck key on its rabbit's foot key chain, and tossed it to clank on the desk. "Take it. If they can start it, they can have it."

Kowalchuck rubbed the back of his neck and exhaled, then picked up his notebook again and flipped to another page. "There is another way you could cooperate. I have a list of names. I'll read it out to you, and all you have to do is nod if you recognize the name. You don't have to say anything." Kowalchuck looked down at his notebook. "Ruby McCann," then looked up again. Ben shook his head. "Jake MacGuigan."

"Never heard of him." Which was strictly true. Ben had filled in shifts pumping gas at the MacGuigans' garage from time to time, and gone fishing or poker-playing with Jake many's the time. So it wouldn't be accurate to say he'd "heard of him."

"Alvin States."

"Oh hell, Corporal, save your breath. You could read out the whole Membertou County phone book, I ain't no damned informer." Ben breathed out the air trapped at the bottom of his trapped lungs. "I guess you better call Legal Aid after all."

* * *

Within about three minutes of picking up her husband from the RCMP station, Bonnie had got the gist of what had happened. Ben was so agitated he was practically flailing around, which was a bit nervous-making: a very agitated, very big man in a very small car. He ranted, "How could I have been so goddamned *stupid*? But, how paranoid do you have to be to imagine the Federal Excise Department'd put together a whole complicated sting operation, just because a few old folks in the hills are making stuff for people who can't afford the liquor store?" He grew quieter. "I dunno. There's somethin' else to it. Somethin's goin' on."

"Maybe it's just something as simple and stupid as – you remember back in psychedelic days, when drugs were first getting around and the police didn't have a clue how or why? Anybody they caught with half a joint in his pocket had to be part of some international anarchist conspiracy, and they'd get a search warrant and trash his place, looking for the secret code."

"I dunno. Maybe. But . . . uh, fact is, I been getting that stuff for years. Why now?" Ben rubbed one summer-freckled paw back and forth across his mouth, as though his knuckles and his mouth were negotiating whether he should say something. "You see, uh . . . that 'cheap, westren vodka' I been buying since way back, and keep a half-watered bottle in the fridge . . . that ain't vodka. Oh, every now and then, when I have to replace the cupboard bottle when the label gets so worn it's obvious. But otherwise, it's local product."

"I know."

"You do?"

"Ben, I was born at night, but it wasn't last night. Even though I drown vodka in cranapple juice and can't tell from the taste, I figured it out a long time ago. I didn't know how often it wasn't vodka, but I figured it wasn't always. And I also figured you wouldn't bring anything in the house that wasn't safe to drink."

"Well, it *is* safe, aren't been much danger of bad moonshine ever since most people started using stainless steel instead of copper. Oh, maybe there's still some idiots in the backwoods of New Brunswick using an old car radiator for a cooling chamber, but mostly . . . Goddamn government says the reason they won't let you make your own liquor, like beer and wine, is they don't want you to get poisoned. Bullshit. Anybody that's careful and knows what they're doing can make safe liquor. The real reason's money. As usual. They make a hell of a lot more money off whiskey tax than beer and wine." Ben's anger ran down for the moment. He muttered, "I shoulda listened to Clyde."

"Clyde?"

"Yeah, he went nuts when them excise agents came into the yard. Barking and snarling and trying to lunge off his line. Smart dog. Smarter'n me. Oh, pull into MacGuigans' for a minute, would you?"

"For the payphone."

"Yeah. Shouldn't be long."

Bonnie pulled into the gas station, parked away from the pumps and watched her husband walk to the payphone under the awning. From the back, his body shape still fit the traditional male ideal of the upside-down wedge, wide shoulders and narrow hips. But his walk was a little stiff. What the ideal-makers hadn't thought of was that when the shoulders were too wide in relation to the hips, it eventually got hard on the lower back and knees. Bonnie had often been unhappy that she was built like a fireplug, but at least it was durable.

Ben was only half a minute at the payphone, then squeezed himself back into the car and nodded at her to carry on homeward. As she started up the old Honda again, she said, "No answer?"

"Oh, yeah. But all I had to say was 'They're lookin'.' Person at the other end said, 'Where?' and I said, 'Everywhere,' and that was that."

Bonnie's perpetual state of curiosity was worse than a teenager's hormones, but she knew better than to ask who 'the person' at the other end of the phone line had been. She also knew, from Ben's description of the conversation, that the person had 'lockdown-and-hideaway' down pretty pat. Maybe a box built into the side of a hill, with turf on the lid, maybe a huge shed so chock full of junk and bric-a-brac it would take the police a month of man-hours to pick through it all.

Ben seemed subdued, chewing on his lower lip. "I'm sorry, Bonnie." But then he was off again. "Goddammit, the whole reason we got laws and law officers is so we can have a decent place to live. But who wants to live in a place where anyone who offers a little hospitality to a couple of half-drowned strangers is a fool?" Then he went quiet again. "Guess that makes me a fool."

"You're not a fool, Ben. Just generous, and trusting."

"Yeah, well, generous and trusting might be cute in a five-year-old, but adults should grow out of it."

"I hope not."

Back home, Bonnie couldn't think of what else to do except go back to what she'd been doing, which was cleaning her own house for a change. She wondered whether they should pour the watered bottle in the fridge down the sink, and the undiluted one in the cupboard, but Ben said, "They already got me. No need to waste their time swearing out a search warrant and mounting a raid." Ben took the piece of paper with the Legal Aid lawyer's name and number down to the phone in their bedroom in the basement, away from the sound of the vacuum. He was down there a long time. By the time he came back up again, Bonnie'd vacuumed the living/dining room, the kitchen, Melissa's room, and even Moyle's and Robbie's and Darcy's rooms, even though they hadn't been slept in since the last time she'd vacuumed. When Ben did come back up, they poured themselves a drink and sat down in the kitchen.

Bonnie said, "Did the lawyer sound any good?"

"Well, sounds like she's fresh out of law school, but pretty energetic. She must've got on it as soon as she got assigned the case, prob'ly before you and me even pulled out of the Mountie parking lot. She's already got me my truck back. They prob'ly couldn't get it started. But, I think maybe we should wait till tomorrow to go pick it up."

Bonnie just nodded. Melissa would be home soon, and they would've had to take her with them instead of leaving her home alone. She was a little young yet for an explanation of why they had to pick up Daddy's pickup from the RCMP.

"And there was, uh . . . the lawyer said something else. She said the Crown prosecutor had told her not to waste her time trying to play the angle that the excise agents didn't have grounds to pull the sting on me. It seems they don't have to tell her what those grounds are, because it's part of a 'ongoing investigation.' They'll just tell her and the magistrate in private, once my case comes to trial . . ."

Ben's weary blue eyes travelled down to the salt and pepper shakers Moyle had made in woodworking class, and he put his hand on the table to move them back and forth a little. Then he looked back up. "Like I said back in the car, Bonnie, there's something weird going on. There's something been happening around here, that I could prob'ly find out if I nosed around, but . . . Any place I go to visit now, I'll likely be tailed, and the cops'll add those names to their list. Not to mention that I'm kinda aggravated, and I'm liable to end up throwing people up against walls if they don't answer my questions, and that won't do anybody any good.

"But you – you can get people to answer questions without them even knowing you asked. And you know a lot of people you could drop in on for a cup of tea, or have a innocent chat with while you're taking a break from cleaning their house."

Bonnie took a sip of her cranapple juice and illegal contraband liquor, and thought about what he was asking her to do. "All right, Ben, I'll see what I can find out."

"Thank you."

* * *

It took about ten days, and about twenty gallons of tea in other people's kitchens, before Bonnie called Ben into her own kitchen and said, "Okay, I think I've found out what's going on, or at least found out how to find out."

"Oh good, thank you. I was wondering if you were ever going to say anything about it."

"I was wondering whether my kidneys were going to give out." Bonnie poured herself a glass of water from the water cooler tap; it'd be a while before she could look a teabag in the face again. They didn't take drinking water from their well anymore, what with gypsum leeching from the strip mines, arsenic from old gold mine tailings, too many old septic systems that'd been built before the days of dishwashers and daily showers – sometimes more than daily for teenagers – and automatic clothes washers in every home. And there were probably a few other sources of poison in the water table that the hoi polloi weren't told about, and Bonnie suspected she probably didn't want to know.

The kitchen water cooler hadn't cost much, a loss-leader from a bottled water company. The Marsdens had bought several of the company's big jugs of water, but hadn't taken back the empties and bought refills. There was a semi-retired couple who ran a Christmas tree U-cut, and they'd accidentally discovered an artesian spring on a part of their property just across the old highway from their house. They'd put in a standing pipe and a tap, and a gravelled mini parking lot, and anyone who wanted to fill up jugs with fresh, clean, pure water just had to turn the tap. Every now and then there'd be an anonymous complaint to the Health Department that the water wasn't safe to drink, word would get around and people would chip in to have the water tested, and it always came out pure. Some people suspected that the anonymous complaints came from one of the stores that sold bottled water, or from one of the bottled water companies. Some people also suspected that the whole free water thing was just a clever promo for the Christmas tree business. But Bonnie didn't think so. Bonnie figured that the old fella didn't like the idea of his neighbours having to go buy something he had an endless, free-flowing supply of.

Bonnie took in and swallowed a large mouthful of water that tasted like water, not chlorine, then said to Ben, "I think I found out more about the community we live in in the last week and a half than almost fifty years before. You know that nice young couple from away who moved into the old Collier place?"

"Yeah. Well, know 'em to see 'em."

"They're in the Witness Protection Program. So, I thought maybe they might be trying to keep up their informant credentials. And old Connie McDermott, Horton's aunt, seems she's tried to sic the Mounties on just about everybody she knows, for everything from downloading online porn to not reporting their Bingo winnings. So, I thought maybe . . . But then . . . Do you know a kid named Billy Vickers?"

"Billy Vickers?" The corners of Ben's mouth and eyebrows crinkled down, which usually meant he was thinking. "No, I don't think so. A kid?"

"Just past the age of Young Offender, unluckily for him. He was arrested a couple of months ago, at a hydroponic marijuana operation up in Mertonville."

"Oh, yeah, I did some work on that place."

"You *what?*"

"Just some porch-fixing and repointing the chimney. I didn't go inside." He raised the teapot in her direction, to ask if she wanted some before refilling his cup. She shook her head.

"Did you know it was a growhouse?"

"Well, nobody *said* it was, but it don't take a genius to figure: two young fellas from the city with no visible means of support renting a place in the country, a buried power cable running from the hydro line but not connected to the meter, and a barn with boarded-up windows but light coming out through the cracks. It was none of my business. But, wait a minute, you said this Billy Vickers was just past the Young Offenders' line . . .?"

"Yeah."

"Well, those two guys at the growhouse were in their mid-twenties, maybe older."

"Billy Vickers didn't live there, he just happened to be there when the police arrived."

"Oh yeah, the gopher. Local kid who ran errands for them. I think they paid him in weed."

"Well, even though his case was in adult court, growing marijuana with intent to traffic, he got off with a conditional sentence and time served." Ben looked a bit surprised at that, as he should. But overall, he was starting to get that 'What's this got to do with the price of eggs?' expression. "The reason they let him off so lightly, was he gave a videotaped confession. A long, videotaped confession."

"I wouldn't've thought a kid that age would have much to confess."

"He wasn't just confessing for himself. It seems that he was confessing for so many other people, some secretary in his lawyer's office, or maybe the RCMP office, thought a cousin who lived around here could make a lot of money selling copies. They're going for two hundred dollars apiece."

"*Two hundred dollars?*"

"They say your name's on the tape."

"Who says?"

"Wanda Burch, over in Butcher's Corners. But that's all she'll say. She never gives anything away."

Ben looked at the ceiling, slowly shaking his head. "Two hundred dollars . . ."

3

Bonnie was tucking Melissa into bed while Ben set up the videotape in the rec room downstairs. Melissa said, "But I want to watch the movie, too."

"It's not a movie you'd like, honey. And you've got school in the morning. Just close your eyes and before you know it, Clyde'll be snuggled up beside you." The last thing Ben did before going to bed was bring Clyde in for the night, or take him for a poop-walk if Clyde hadn't wanted to go back outside after he'd had his supper. Nobody had told Clyde that Floyd had always slept on Melissa's bed; Clyde had just naturally done it since the first night they brought him home from Death Row.

When Bonnie got downstairs, Ben was sitting tensely in his oversized, worn La-Z-Boy, with a tall glass of ice and water and actual 'cheap westren vodka.' They'd used up what Ben had on hand of the other stuff, and both agreed that he should wait at least a while before thinking of getting some more.

Ben handed her the remote, saying, "My hand's all sweaty." She sat down and pressed Play. Wanda Burch had told her that it wasn't the whole tape. Whoever made the copies had skipped past a bunch of preliminaries like ". . . in the presence of his lawyer . . ." The TV flickered for awhile, then came up with a picture from an odd, high angle, like a camera mounted on a ceiling corner. It was a small room with industrial-green walls and a metal desk. Sitting behind the desk was a skinny boy with thin, blonde hair that was neither short nor long, and geeky, black-framed glasses. In front of it sat a man and woman in their thirties. Bonnie said, "You recognize Billy Vickers?"

"Well, that's the gopher all right, so if that's Billy Vickers . . ."

"And the other two are the two drowned rats?"

"Yeah. Her hair was longer and a different colour, but that's them." His tone of voice suggested they were very lucky they were just pictures on a screen. Or maybe Ben was the lucky one, since the law wasn't likely to take kindly to what he'd be likely to do if they were in his home in person.

The female agent put a spiral notebook on the desk and said, *"I have a list of names here, Billy . . ."*

Ben muttered, "They always do."

". . . and you don't have to say anything if you don't want to. If you just nod your head when you recognize a name, that will be enough for us to tell the judge you were cooperative. Of course, if you choose to give us more information than that, we'll be able to tell the judge you were very cooperative."

Billy Vickers said, in a tightened-high, nervous voice, *"You know I want to be as corropative as I can, Marion."*

Ben said, "Marion? I wonder what in hell her real name is. Or if she can remember."

Bonnie said, "Ssh!" Ben had always been the first to complain when someone else talked to the TV so much no one else could tell what was going on.

The female agent started through her list of names, looking up for Billy Vickers's reaction between each. A few of the names Bonnie recognized, at least vaguely. But the kid didn't seem to, and seemed to be becoming even more nervous, as his opportunities for being "corropative" slipped by. Then the agent read, *"Ben Marsden."*

Billy Vickers almost smiled, and said with a kind of relief in his voice, *"Oh, yeah."*

'Marion' said, *"Ben Marsden?"*

Billy Vickers said, *"Yeah, Big Ben Marsden. He was up at the growhouse a few times, doing odd jobs. That's how he makes his living, doing odd jobs, but I think it's just a front. One day, after Big Ben pulled out the driveway, one of the growhouse guys said, 'That big dumb country boy's got his fingers in every scheme in Membertou County . . ."*

Ben snorted, "I wish."

". . . and he always had a pint of moonshine in his toolbox."

"Do you think he has a still?"

"Oh, I wouldn't be surprised if he has five or six stills, dotted here and there around the county." Billy took off his glasses, blinking, and wiped them with his shirttail. *"Probably running truckloads into the city, for taverns to mix in with their legal vodka and gin. I mean, there's a lot of money to be made that way, isn't there?"*

The male agent said, *"That's right, Billy."*

The female agent said, *"Does Ben Marsden have a growhouse, too?"*

"Oh, I don't know about a growhouse, but he's likely got a few acres of woods behind his place. All those old guys do. That's probably where he grows it."

Bonnie said, "The helicopter!"

Ben said, "Huh?"

"That morning, the helicopter you heard going back and forth over our woodlot! They were looking for Ben Marsden's marijuana plantation!"

"Holy Jesus Crippled Christ. How many tens of thousands of dollars did they spend, on agents and helicopters and what-else, just to catch one guy with half a pint of moonshine in his barn."

They both turned their attention to the TV again. The agents seemed to have finished with Ben Marsden and had gone on to other names. Ben waved his hand downward and said, "You might as well shut it off, I'm done. Done but good." But, in the two seconds it took Bonnie to find the Stop button, something happened that made Ben say, "Wait a minute. Just, uh, run it back a little bit, okay? Then play it back."

She did. What came out was a couple of names Billy Vickers

didn't respond to, and then: *"Jack Burton."*

Billy Vickers said, *"Oh, yeah. He's the boss of it all. He fronts the money for the growhouses, hires the guys to run them —"*

"Okay," Ben said from that long-distance place, "that's enough."

As the machine whirred its rewinding, Bonnie said, "Who's Jack Burton? Somebody you know?"

"Not hardly. Just enough to know that poor dumb kid would've been safer staying in jail."

"Why? Is Jack Burton innocent, too?"

"No. From what little I know of Jack Burton, I'd say he isn't innocent of just about anything you can imagine. And probably a few things you can't."

* * *

The night before Ben's preliminary hearing — which was going to be the only hearing, because he was going to plead guilty of possession, and his lawyer and the Crown were agreed on the facts — Bonnie was just drifting off when Ben whispered, "Bonnie? You still awake?"

Bonnie murmured, "Again?" partly in surprise, partly in delight, partly in doubt that she had any energy left.

"Uh, no, sorry, I ain't nineteen anymore . . ."

"Felt like it to me."

"There's just, uh, something I think we should talk about."

Bonnie rolled over onto her back and turned her head toward him. Ben was lying on his side facing her, propped up on one elbow. Not that she could see anything but vague shapes; the only light was moonlight through the window high on the wall.

Ben settled his free hand on her belly. She could feel the calluses and the reassuring weight through her worn-thin, summer nightgown. Ben said, in a soft, close-by, bed voice, "You know, like my lawyer said, the sentence'll most likely be a five-hundred-dollar fine or two weeks in jail?"

"Uh-huh."

"Bonnie . . . We can't afford five hundred dollars."

"We've got seven hundred and thirty-two in the bank."

"That's for next month's mortgage, and the power bill. If we get a month behind, or start borrowing to pay the bills, we'll just keep falling back, until eventually we'll lose this place, and then where're we gonna go?"

Bonnie realized what he was saying, and bolted upright like a jack-in-the-box. "You can't go to jail!"

"I sure as hell don't want to. Only jail-time I ever done was overnighters when I was a kid, and I didn't much like it. But a two-week sentence – with mandatory release I'd only serve ten days, unless I punch a guard or something. Five hundred dollars is more'n I'd make in ten days of scrounging odd jobs."

Bonnie lay back down, on her side facing him, and put her hand on his bare shoulder. "Ben, it's been almost thirty years since we went ten days in a row without seeing each other. Except that few months way back, when you had to go out west to find work."

"Oh, we'll see each other. I won't be on the far side of the moon. They got visiting hours. Lawyer said they might even let me serve my sentence in the little Mountie lock-up in Raddallton, and that's only a twenty-minute drive."

"'Visiting hours' isn't quite what I meant. I should've said ten *nights*."

"Well . . ." Ben's hand came up to the side of her head and curled its fingers in her curls. "Not that way-back, when they screwed up your surgery and had to restitch you, you were out of commission for a lot longer'n ten days. We survived."

"That was different."

"Why?"

"Because *I* was the one who was out of commission."

They both laughed, and Ben butted his forehead against hers. It was a desperate kind of laughter, though. There seemed to be a dark weight pressing down between Bonnie's shoulder blades, and not a reassuring one. Ben rolled away from her onto his back, and seemed to be deciding whether to say something.

Bonnie waited.

Ben eventually said, "Hell, I probably won't even notice the first week or so. I'll be busy going through withdrawal."

"Withdrawal?"

"Bonnie, I'm an alcoholic."

"That's ridiculous! I haven't seen you falling-down drunk in years!"

"I haven't been. I just been, uh, like they say on the dog-food labels, 'basic maintenance.' Like the kid said on the tape, I always got a pint in my toolbox. Helps to keep me from losing my patience. If I go too long without a nip, my hands start to shake."

Bonnie let that settle into her, and considered whether it could be true, considering how much time Ben spent out of her sight, away on jobs, or working in the barn or the yard. Even when they were both in the kitchen, or watching TV, he naturally had to step away to the bathroom from time to time. She said, "How much do you drink, Ben?"

"Oh, maybe a quart of the good stuff a week. Some of the old fellas around here'd call me a piker. But, even still . . ." Ben let out a chuckle that didn't sound entirely domesticated. Bonnie was going to ask him what he found funny about what he was telling her, then realized he'd just realized *still's* other meaning as he'd said it. ". . . it's probably a good thing I'll have to go cold turkey in a place with bars in the windows and locks on the doors. Who knows, I might come out a different man."

"I never wanted a different man, Ben."

* * *

The main courtroom in the Raddallton courthouse was all wood-panelled, and not the kind of wood-panelling people put in their rec rooms. Bonnie was sitting in the first row behind the wooden fence, while her husband stood on the other side. The round-faced, wispy-haired judge looked and sounded a bit like Clarence, the apprentice angel in *It's A Wonderful Life*. "The court appreciates, Mr. Marsden, that you have been very cooperative in pleading guilty, thus saving the court a good deal of time, and the taxpayers a good deal of money.

"But you have been very *un*cooperative by refusing to divulge the names of your associates. The Crown and your defence have agreed upon a joint recommendation for sentence. But I am not bound by their agreement." The judge's face and voice transformed from Clarence the Angel to Lionel Barrymore's spiteful Mr. Potter. "You may be a very small fish in a very large pond, Mr. Marsden, but it's a scummy pond in need of cleaning up. I sentence you to pay a two-thousand-dollar fine or spend two months in jail."

Bonnie heard intakes of breath all around her. Even the Crown prosecutor looked surprised. Bonnie was blinking and gaping around, trying to clear her vision. This wasn't a movie.

The judge waved his black-robed arm and said, "Next case."

4

A sixty-day sentence would be forty days with good behaviour. It soon seemed like it was going to be the longest forty days in Bonnie's life. The kids helped out as much as they could. Robbie came home on the weekends from community college in Truro, and Darcy came home from Halifax on 'waitress weekends' – two days mid-week when the tips weren't nearly as good as Friday night through Sunday. Moyle phoned more than a few times from the oil patch in Alberta, just to chat, more times than he would usually call in the course of a year. On days when Darcy or Robbie was home to look after Melissa, Bonnie could drive to the city to visit Ben in the provincial jail. Melissa was told that Daddy was working a temporary job in New Brunswick, so wouldn't be home for awhile.

The weather turned out to be as generous as the kids. There was a late autumn to make up for the miserable spring that had made the garden go in late. So Bonnie was able to keep herself busy stewing tomato sauce for the freezer, canning green beans with the dreaded pressure cooker, bottling crabapple jelly. But no matter how much she tired herself out with work and cooking, she still woke up in the middle of the night with uneasy feelings.

The one blessing to the situation that Bonnie kept reminding herself of was that she didn't have to worry about a worry that probably plagued most women whose husbands, or brothers, or sons were spending a few weeks in jail. The worry was that short-timers tended to get victimized by long-timers, who would beat up, bully and harass them to get their visitors to smuggle in drugs. That was not likely to happen to Big Ben Marsden. Or at least, the first fool who tried it would serve as a pulped example to the others. Especially since Ben would be grouchy with alcohol withdrawal. The first few times Bonnie visited Ben, she could see he had the sweats and nervous tics, but it seemed to settle down after that. If Ben truly was an alcoholic, his 'basic maintenance' certainly wasn't high dosage. Bonnie had seen heavy-duty alcoholics drying out, and this wasn't that.

Even though Bonnie was quite sure Ben's size and rough experience meant she didn't have the worry other jail-widows had, she was aware that nobody's invulnerable. But as the days went by, his face and hands through the visiting-room grill showed no signs of scrapes or bruises, and he never said anything about having to deal with any trouble. Not that he would.

Even though the autumn stretched on longer than usual, there were signs that winter was definitely on the way. Driving by Dave Chambers's place, Bonnie noticed that the set of bright blue steel car ramps that sat by his garage all summer had been put away. Dave drove a salt truck for the Highways Department in the winter, and in the summer and fall made side-money by undercoating other people's vehicles with hot oil, to protect them from road salt corrosion.

Another sign was that virtually all the birds had gone, either south or into the deep woods. All except the crows, of course. Standing at her kitchen window watching three crows play aerial tag, Bonnie remembered some old person saying, "If men grew feathers and sprouted wings, very few would be clever enough to be crows."

On the thirty-third day of the long forty, Bonnie heard on the news that an as-yet-unidentified young man had died in a terrible accident, on a back road up near Mertonville. His car had caught on fire, exploded its gas tank and burned him to death. Bonnie clucked her tongue and murmured, "What a sin." On the thirty-sixth day, the news told her that the young man had been identified by dental records. William Arnold "Billy" Vickers.

That day, Bonnie was scheduled to pick up Darcy from the noon bus in Raddallton, even though it was a Friday. Robbie had something on at college he couldn't get out of, so Darcy had volunteered to give up her good-tips weekend and wouldn't take no for an answer. A fog had come in off the bay, so it was slow going into town, and there was always some idiot from away who thought turning his brights on would help him see through fog. In the gas station/bus station parking lot, Bonnnie switched off the ignition, given the price of gas, but left the tape player on. That turned out to be a mistake. She had enough trouble not getting teary these days, without that lilting, working-class tenor singing:

Don't you worry, darling, don't you know I'll be there,
I'll be there, when all your dreams are broken . . .

The passenger door suddenly cracked open, and Bonnie jumped and let out a squawk. It was just Darcy, throwing her overnight bag into the back seat and climbing in. "Are you all right, Mom?"

"Yeah, you just surprised me is all." Bonnie turned on the ignition, wiped her eyes, and started off. "It's so misty out there, I didn't even see the bus come in."

"Not just out there. You sure you're all right?"

"Fine. I just . . . was listening to an old song by your dad's cousin, and it made me sort of . . . foolish."

"Dad's cousin?"

"Oh, a silly thing your father likes to say. You see, your father's great-grandfather, Harold Marsden, immigrated from the capital of Ireland. And Gerald Marsden, of Gerry and the Pacemakers, was born in the capital of Ireland and stayed there."

"Dublin?"

"Liverpool. It's an old joke, 'cause there were so many Irish dockworkers and cleaning ladies in Liverpool. Guess I'm keeping up the Marsden tradition."

"You're more than just a cleaning lady, Mom."

"So was everybody that ever mopped floors for a living."

Now that they were clear of town traffic, Bonnie glanced across at her daughter – her only daughter up until six years ago, when Melissa proved that the tubal ligation after Robbie didn't have a lifetime warranty. Darcy's hair was black these days, but Bonnie was in no position to sermonize about people ruining their hair with dye jobs, given all those years at the credit union when she'd switched from colour to colour, depending on which shade was deemed more elegantly businesslike that season. Since it had only been a few days since she'd last seen Darcy, Bonnie left off the ritual of clucking about how thin she looked, to which Darcy would inevitably reply something like, *I work in a restaurant, Mom! I can't count how many untouched leftovers I scoff up every night!*

Bonnie said, "Did you get a chance to visit your father lately?"

"Yeah, just yesterday. He said you didn't have to bother going in to visit him tomorrow, since he's getting out on Tuesday. I don't think he meant it."

"How'd he seem?"

Darcy shrugged. "You know Dad. Almost as bad as you for complaining. 'If you can't change it, don't bitch about it.'"

Bonnie laughed, but not hard enough to explain the tears stinging the corners of her eyes. She let the moment settle, then said, "Did you hear about that poor kid who got burned up in the car fire around here?"

"Yeah." Darcy shuddered. "What a horrible way to go."

"Well, I shouldn't say a 'kid,' I guess, more like a young man, just a couple of years younger than you."

"I'm still a kid."

"Anyway, they said who he was on the news this morning. Billy Vickers. He was the one on that videotape that got the excise agents chasing your father, with the list of names."

"Jesus!"

"No, he wasn't on the list. But there was someone else who was. Someone who made your father say, 'That poor, dumb kid would be better off staying in jail.' It took me awhile to remember the name. Jack Burton."

"Who's Jack Burton?"

"I don't know, and your father says he hardly knows him. But just the name was enough to give your dad the chills."

Bonnie could feel her daughter looking at her while she watched the road. After a moment, Darcy said, "Mom, I know whenever something weird happens in Membertou County, you've gotta get out your microfying glass and your deerstalker hat. But don't you think you've got enough to worry about just now, without worrying about some dead kid you never even met?"

Bonnie took that in and let it lie. When they got home, Darcy headed into the house while Bonnie headed back up the driveway to the mailbox. There was the power bill, right on schedule, unlike Nova Scotia Power's storm-blackout repairs. And there was another envelope, standard size and standard white, but very strange. It was addressed to "Ms. B. Marsden," which wasn't all that strange, but the embossed return address was the Wild Rose Credit Union in Alberta. Bonnie opened it right there beside the mailbox and skimmed the letter inside, then read it through again. It still said what it had said the first time, and she still felt like she'd been whacked on the back of the head with a rubber mallet.

Bonnie drifted dazedly down to the house and in. Darcy was putting the kettle on, and said over her shoulder, "Jeez, Mom, I thought you were just going up to the mailbox. Did you get lost?" and then caught a look of her mother's face. "What's happened?"

"Uh, this letter, from the Wild Rose Credit Union, in Alberta." Bonnie held it up and waggled it. "They're offering me a job in their loans department. Starting salary of forty-three thousand dollars."

"Forty-three thousand?"

"Plus benefits!" Darcy literally jumped up and down, so Bonnie figured she could, too. But a little adult perspective seemed called for. "Well, they haven't really offered me the job yet, just offered to fly me out for an interview. But if they're already talking salary, I guess they're pretty serious."

"I guess!"

"They say I should call them collect, so I'll call 'em Monday."

"You could call 'em today, with the time change and all."

"No, never make business calls when you're surprised and excited. Wait till you calm down." Bonnie pursed her mouth at herself. "Did that sound too much like mother patronizing daughter? Or matronizing."

"No, it makes sense. Just like calling guys."

"Guys are supposed to call *you*."

"It's a different century, Mom."

The kettle whistled and Darcy filled the teapot. Bonnie could stomach tea again; any kind of comfort over the last five weeks was welcome. They sat down across the kitchen table from each other, the same kid-proof Formica and steel-tube table they'd sat at thousands of times, on the same chairs whose plastic upholstery Ben had replaced several times. It crossed Bonnie's mind that the chair Darcy Longlegs was sitting on might be the same one they used to stack telephone books on, so she could reach the table.

Bonnie said, "There's something really weird about this letter. I don't know how they got my résumé. I sent it out to a lot of places, but only places within commuting distance of here. Even a long commute. But not as long as Alberta. I don't know anybody in Alberta."

"Except Moyle."

"This doesn't seem like something Moyle would do. Sounds more like something you would do, or Robbie."

"Well, it sure as hell wasn't me."

After the first cup of tea, it was time to walk down the hill and meet the schoolbus. Melissa seemed a little sullen when she got off the bus, but five-year-olds had their moods, unlike forty-five-year-olds. As the female half of the Marsden family walked back up along the gravel shoulder and nominally paved road, Bonnie looked around at the neighbourhood – nothing fancy, but

40

most of the houses had yards that town or city people would call huge. She hadn't taken much notice of the outside world lately. Although the leaves were all down, and the woods belonged to the pine trees again, it was still surprisingly warm. Julie's horse corral had a new pony in it.

Darcy said, "How was school today?"

"Teacher made me take a timeout for beating up George Stirling."

Darcy, with a barely contained laugh in her voice, said, "Why'd you beat up George Stirling?"

"'Cause he said," Melissa's voice shifted into the timeless singsong of schoolyard nastiness, "*Sissy Melissy, her daddy is a jailbird,*" and then back into her own voice, "What's a jailbird?"

Bonnie could see Darcy looking at her over Melissa's head, unsure of what to say. Bonnie said, "It's just a silly name for someone who made a mistake and had to take a long timeout. Are they gonna let you bring one of your rabbits into school next week?"

"Yes! Today Mandy brung in her chameleon, next week's my turn."

"Which one are you going to take?" As Melissa rattled on about the pros and cons of the white one versus the spotted one, Bonnie caught Darcy casting her mother a saucy look. The look said, *And how many times when* I *was a kid did you fake me out like that?*

After supper, when the phone rates were lower, Bonnie called Moyle's cell phone and got his answering service, so figured he must be out on the job, or however they phrased that in the oil rig world. She left a message and was surprised when he called back only a few minutes later. She could hear the sounds of heavy machinery behind him, so he was still at work. The first thing he said was, "Are you all right, Mom?"

"Yes, fine. I didn't mean to scare you. I just –" She told him about the letter from Alberta, and that since he was the only person in Alberta who'd ever heard of her . . .

Moyle's big-chested voice boomed through the phone even

louder than usual, trying to hear himself above the machines. "Mom, I wouldn't know the Wild Rose Credit Union from a hole in the ground, and we got a lotta holes in the ground up here. But, hey, if they're gonna fly you out, I'll take some time off and meet you. Book another seat for Dad and I'll cover it. I, uh, got a lot of frequent-flyer points."

Bonnie wasn't sure if that last part was actually true. There was always a bit of awkwardness around the fact that he earned more in six months than both his parents in a year. But she let it stand and thanked him and let him go back to work.

That left her other son as a possibility. Robbie had always spent a lot of time going to all sorts of places on the Internet. She called his cramped, student studio apartment in Truro and found him there, though not all there. He sounded like he was in the middle of some complicated school assignment, or some other kind of complication. Bonnie explained as briefly as she could, and Robbie said, "Sorry, Mom, I know your curiosity will drive you crazy, but it wasn't me. And, uh, sorry, but just now –"

"I know. It sounds like you're in the middle of something. Talk to you soon."

After Melissa's bedtime and some cribbage with Darcy, Bonnie yawned her way to bed but couldn't get to sleep. It gnawed at her that she couldn't think up any other possibility of who had sent her résumé to Alberta. And her thinking kept being interrupted by horrible images of frail-haired, thick-spectacled Billy Vickers screaming as his car burst into flame around him. She was sure the two things couldn't have the remotest connection to each other. It was just that she'd happened to learn about them on the same day.

Bonnie tried to push away the horrible images by concentrating on the maddening mystery of who had sent her résumé. And then the name of the Wild Rose Credit Union clicked with another name: Rose Coffin. Not that the names were anything but coincidence, but the click brought up a real possibility. When young Rose Coffin was divorcing her much older, jailed husband, she must've had to deal with financial institutions all across the country, ferreting through his rabbit warren of numbered companies, hidden investments and cheque-kiting accounts. Although Rose had been in 4-H with Moyle way back when, she and Bonnie hadn't exactly been in constant contact over the years. But what contact they'd had had been in pretty intense situations. Some would say, and Rose's knife-edged upbringing would make her one of them, that Rose owed Bonnie.

With at least one possible solution to the résumé mystery in mind, Bonnie let her mind drift to what the new job would mean. She would be making decisions again, decisions that had more effect on people's lives than deciding whether to use Mr. Clean or Pine-sol on their bathroom floor. She'd be wearing new dresses and suits to work again, instead of old T-shirts and sweatpants – well, that would mean pantyhose again, but nothing was perfect. Melissa would be wearing new clothes to school, and the schools in Alberta were said to be much better than Nova Scotia. They could buy a new car – they'd been worried about what they were going to do when the baling wire and chewing gum holding the old Honda together finally gave out. And Ben could buy a new truck; no sales tax in Alberta. With all Ben's basic handyman skills and the endless building boom in Alberta, he could easily find a real job out there, and one that would pay three times as much as here even if he could find a job here. Bonnie drifted off to sleep with a smile on her face.

In the morning, Bonnie left for the city some while earlier than needed to get her to the jail on time. Instead of going to the new four-lane highway, she took the old winding two-lane. As she crested a hill, she saw the pseudo-old greenstone mansion that had once belonged to John and Rose MacPherson. That had been Bonnie's Cleaning Service's first-ever job, and the first time her housecleaning had uncovered a crime that the police thought had just been a tragic accident.

The new owners of the mansion had put up a tall privacy fence between it and Ashland Stables, the only asset Rose had been able to hang onto. Bonnie turned into the Ashland Stables driveway, pulled in beside the little pickup truck parked in front of the mini-home and climbed out. At the other end of the parking lot was a corral where several small-sized horses and people were riding in a circle, probably a Saturday Morning Pony Club. Bonnie was about to head that way, when a voice off to her right called, "Hello!" Bonnie turned in that direction. Rose Coffin was standing in the doorway of the mini-home, looking perfectly elegant in an old sweatshirt and jeans. "Are you looking for – ? Bonnie! I thought you were . . ."

"You thought I was a customer. Sorry to disappoint you."

"Don't be silly. Come on in."

Rose held the door as Bonnie stepped inside. There were stacks of receipts and a calculator on the kitchen table. Bonnie said, "Oh, if I'm interrupting your –"

"You ain't interrupting, believe me. Nothing I don't want interrupted." Rose cleared back the papers in front of one of the two kitchen chairs. "Would you like a cup of coffee?"

"Maybe half a cup, thanks. I'm just on my way into the city to, uh . . ."

"To visit Ben." Of course Rose would pick up any news kicking around about Ben; she had good reason to care. "How's he doing?"

"Oh, as well as can be expected. He's getting out Tuesday."

"That's great." Bonnie watched Rose at the kitchen counter dealing with the coffeepot and cups. There'd always been an easy-flowing grace to Rose's movements, as though even the most mundane operation was an unconscious dance. Well, not so graceful when she was a puking-drunk teenager, but otherwise . . . Rose had always put Bonnie in mind of a wild deer. For all their daintiness and delicateness, deer were so much stronger than they looked. And Bonnie knew for a certainty that this one wasn't about to freeze in anybody's headlights.

Rose had to've been born with that grace, because it certainly didn't come from her upbringing. It made it hard to keep your eyes off her. The graceful creature said over her shoulder, "You know, I think it stinks what that judge did to Ben. Friggin' magistrates think they're God. I don't think Corporal Kowalchuck had anything to do with that shithead sentence."

"Probably not." Rose nodded at the confirmation, and Bonnie suspected she would've seen at least a small smile in the nod, if Rose's face hadn't been turned toward the coffee and the counter. Bonnie wondered if Rose knew that she knew the reason Rose would want to have good things about Corporal Kowalchuck agreed upon, and why Rose could only guess at what he might say, think or do. Probably not. Bonnie's eyes drifted over to a corner of the kitchen, where two cardboard boxes were standing on the floor. One of the flaps was open, so she could see they were cases of wine. They weren't there because Rose threw a lot of parties.

Rose brought the coffee to the table and sat down. Bonnie told her about the credit union in Alberta, and why she thought Rose might've been the one who sent them her résumé.

"It wasn't me, Bonnie. I'da maybe done it if I thought of it, but I didn't. Oh, but no, even if I'd thought of it, I likely wouldn'ta done it. 'Cause I'da never thought you were thinking of moving away."

"Well, nobody around here's been offering me that kind of job."

They chatted awhile longer about this and that, and then Bonnie went back to her car and left Rose to go back to her accounts. As Bonnie pulled back onto the highway, she had to face the fact that everyone she could even remotely suspect of being the one who'd got her name to the Wild Rose Credit Union had drawn a blank. She muttered to herself something her mother used to mutter, on extremely rare occasions, "This is getting desperate-strange."

But that mood got pushed aside by another inspiration of what the job would mean. They could buy Melissa a computer, with a broadband hook-up. It might just be a toy for Melissa at first, but the skills she would learn by playing with it would give her a good boost into schoolwork and eventually work-work. Bonnie was a little rusty, after two years away from working with a keyboard and mouse, but she was sure she could get enough of it back to teach Melissa the basics. Melissa was bright and quick and her in-skull hard-drive wasn't cluttered up with old files. By the time she was eight or nine, she would probably be teaching Bonnie things.

A cautionary voice in Bonnie's mind told her not to count her chickens. Bonnie replied to it that the Wild Rose Credit Union egg had arrived with beak holes already showing through the shell.

At the ridiculously euphemistic Central Nova Scotia Correctional Facility – right up there with calling an old folks' home a senior citizens' residence – Bonnie went through the registration routine and then was ushered to the visitation area. It was a large, bright room that smelled slightly of nervous sweat and disinfectant. A counter with chairs in front of it ran the width of the room, with cubicle walls every few feet and a telephone handset hanging from each right-hand wall. Behind the cubicle walls and running the length of the room was a sheet of thick plexiglass that might've been a mirror if there was no one in the room, since it showed the same cubicles, counter and telephones.

Bonnie sat down at an empty cubicle, and a moment later Ben sat down across from her, on the other side of the glass. Ben was wearing the same green work pants, shirt and white T-shirt as all the other prisoners. Some wore them buttoned to the neck and cuffs, some wore the overshirts open, with the sleeves rolled up over their biceps. Ben wore his partly buttoned and the sleeves rolled halfway up his forearms. She suspected that was partly because the sleeves weren't long enough. His face and hands had grown paler over his five-and-a-half weeks inside, and the freckles showed more without the blending red-brown from sun and wind. His hands weren't only paler, but cleaner. Not that he'd habitually come to the supper table with dirty hands, but no amount of end-of-the-day scrubbing would take out the traces of oil and earth and roof tar embedded in the cracks in his calluses and under his fingernails.

Ben picked up his phone and Bonnie picked up hers and they started the visit with the formula they'd fallen into since the first time they'd looked through that glass at each other. Ben said, "You all right?"

"Pretty good. You?"

"Yeah."

She told him the amazing story of the Wild Rose Credit Union. When she was done, it seemed to take him a while to register it all. He said, "Alberta? What, uh, what do the kids think of us maybe packing up and moving to Alberta?"

"Oh, Moyle and Darcy and Robbie are all old enough they have their own lives now. And Melissa's young enough to adjust."

"I guess . . ."

There was a pause, the kind of apparently odd pause that Bonnie had long ago got used to from visiting people in hospitals. There was so much to say, and so much to take in, that sometimes you couldn't think of what to say. The best thing to do was just let the silence lie for awhile. Then Bonnie said, "Did you hear about Billy Vickers?"

"You mean about his 'accident'?"

Bonnie could hear the quote marks through the phone. "You don't think it was an accident?"

"All's I know's what I read in the papers. But, you remember back when we were watching that videotape, there were some people on that list that made me say the kid'd be safer-off staying in jail."

"It wasn't 'some people.' Just one name. Jack Burton."

Ben glanced from side-to-side, as though the cubicle walls had ears, then leaned forward and hissed into the phone, "You don't have to *shout* it. Damn, I shoulda known your jackdaw memory'd remember more'n just in general."

Bonnie leaned forward and hiss-whispered, "Who's Jack Burton?"

"Oh, just a guy who owns an autobody shop in Dartmouth. And probably a few other businesses that don't figure in the yellow pages. I only met him the once, and he scared the bejesus out of me."

"Out of *you*? What did he do?"

"Nothing. He was just one of a bunch of guys sitting around having a beer."

"Then how did he – ?"

"Look, Bonnie, if you play around the edges of the law, you'll meet a lot of stupid guys, and a few smart guys, and some tough guys, and some crazy guys. But every now and then you'll run across a guy who's smart and tough and crazy. All you can do with somebody like that is stay the hell away from him, and hope he gets caught or shot before he runs over somebody you care about."

"And that's why you didn't say anything about him to the police."

Ben's head went back on his shoulders, and there was that long-distance look again, as though she'd just revealed herself as someone dialling from another planet. It occurred to her that the long-distance look had been occurring more frequently, ever since she'd lost her job and had been spending more time around home and around him.

Whatever it was that had caused that look this time, Ben let it pass and went on with, "Billy Vickers should've known better."

"He was just a scared kid, with the police twisting him around like a rubber doll."

"Makes no difference. People pay for their mistakes. I made a mistake and I'm paying for it. Billy Vickers made a bigger mistake and he paid for it. That's all there is to it."

"You don't mean that."

"I do. It's a different world, Bonnie, with different rules. I been living in that world for almost six weeks now, and believe me, we don't want any part of it. We pay people like Corporal Kowalchuck good money to deal with it for us."

"Corporal Kowalchuck!"

"Huh?"

"He's from out west. Maybe he's the one who got my name in at the Wild Rose Credit Union. It wouldn't be the first time he did us a favour without telling us. And maybe he feels bad about . . ." Bonnie glanced around at the place they were in. ". . . you know . . ."

"Yeah, maybe he does."

There was another one of those pauses, and then Ben said, "What'd I get Melissa for her birthday?"

"Oh, a few years ago we would've called it something out of James Bond, but now it's just a ten-dollar kid's toy. It's a pen with a chip in it that works like a tape recorder. It only records about thirty seconds at a time, but it's amazingly accurate. I have to take it away from her when I tuck her in, or she'd be talking to herself all night."

Ben chuckled, then said, "What's it look like?"

Bonnie was about to ask him why, then realized it was so he wouldn't say 'What's that?' about the present he'd given her. "Well, it's a bit fatter than most ballpoint pens – good for little kids' hands. And it's mostly purple plastic, with a bit of neon green and orange swirls."

"I should be able to recognize that."

They talked a while longer about nothing in particular, just the kind of conversation they might have while putting supper together. Ben seemed to like hearing any details of what was going on at home, the more mundane the better. Bonnie groused about the fact that she hadn't been able to find good ketchup on the store shelves lately, just the watery kind. She said, "I guess Nova Scotia's at the bottom of the food chain, and rural Nova Scotia's the bottom of the bottom."

Ben said, "Maybe, or maybe it's 'cause . . . The stores around home seem to have this philosophy. If you stock two brands of something and one brand sells out and the other doesn't sell, it'd be foolish to order in more of the sold-out brand, 'cause people'd buy it and you'd still be stuck with the stuff nobody wants to buy."

Bonnie laughed and said, "You may be right." Then she looked at her watch. "I better be getting home. Next time I see you, it'll be outside."

"Yeah, uh, take care till then," and they both hung up their phones. They gave each other a kiss through the air, then both stood up and went their separate ways.

On an off chance, Bonnie detoured through Raddallton on her way home and found that Corporal Kowalchuck was actually in his office instead of out on the road. He didn't seem at all reluctant to push aside the paperwork on his desk. She'd heard that paperwork was the curse and bane of a policeman's existence. She said, "Funny, when I saw Rose this morning, she was doing her paperwork, too, and said she didn't mind being interrupted."

A complicated flicker crossed Corporal Kowalchuck's face, at the fact that he and Rose were doing the same thing at the same time. He said flatly, as he said most things, "You saw Rose?"

"Just for a minute. I just dropped in to ask her something."

"How'd she seem?"

"Okay, I guess. Seems lonely."

"Oh." Corporal Kowalchuck looked away from her. "Oh. Well, um . . . Oh." It was a very complicated 'Oh.' That Rose seemed lonely was bound to be good news to him in a way, but a very sad way. Corporal Kowalchuck definitely knew that Bonnie and Ben were the only other people in Membertou County who knew about him and Rose, and their impossible situation.

It had been barely a year since Corporal Kowalchuck, Detachment Commander of the local RCMP, had put Rose's husband away for murder. It wasn't until a few months after that, and after Rose's divorce, that Corporal Kowalchuck and Rose Coffin had actually and accidentally become acquainted – very well-acquainted. But how many people were going to believe that story? So they had to stay away from each other until a lot more time had passed, or until one of them drifted away with somebody else. Bonnie didn't personally believe the second possibility was going to happen, but people get lonely.

Bonnie said, "The reason I dropped in on Rose was to ask her the same question I came to ask you. You see . . ." Bonnie told him about the Wild Rose Credit Union, and how she was flummoxed about who might've got her résumé to Alberta. "But, you're from out west, you must know a lot of people out there. And it wouldn't be the first time you'd done us a favour without advertising."

"Bonnie, it's true I grew up on the prairies, and most of my family's still there, but Winnipeg is eight hundred miles from Calgary. The only people I know in Alberta are officers who took their training the same time I did, and got posted out there."

"Oh. I guess I just did a 'You're from Toronto, you must know my cousin George.'"

"More or less. Well, I'm happy for your new job and all –"

"It's not for sure yet."

" – but I don't know what I'm going to tell the Superintendent when I start solving half the crimes I used to."

"I doubt that. But, speaking of crimes, there's a lot of people saying they don't think Billy Vickers's car catching fire was an accident."

"Oh, an old beater like that, it could've been a lot of things: faulty wiring, leaky gas tank . . ."

"But you don't think so."

Corporal Kowalchuck didn't exactly go long-distance on her, since he just about always was. And his long-distance was different from Ben's, like he was monitoring his own transmissions. "What I might think and what I can prove aren't always the same thing."

"So Jack Burton gets away with it."

There was the tiniest of pauses, then: "Who?"

"Oh, just a name I heard some people say. People like Billy Vickers."

The dark eyes focussed straight on Bonnie, and any trace of 'maybe' disappeared from the voice. "Forget you ever heard it."

"So you *do* know who Jack Burton is."

"Enough to know that if you've come within a mile of him, you've come too close. Leave him to us, we'll get him eventually."

"After he's burned to death how many more screwed-up kids?"

"And maybe a few nice, middle-aged ladies with kids of their own. I'm serious, Bonnie. If my detachment is the one that finally puts together a case against Jack Burton, I'll be sleeping with a shotgun beside my bed. Understood?"

"Understood."

"Good." With that resolved, a tiny wrinkle that crept into one of the corporal's eyebrows might mean he was now thinking about something else. "So, um, what's Ben going to do in Alberta?"

"We haven't had much chance to talk about it yet, but he's getting out on Tuesday –"

"That's good."

" – so we will then. But he'll for sure find it easier to get work in Alberta than around here."

The little wrinkle in Corporal Kowalchuck's left eyebrow crept over into the right one as well, as though maybe he was missing something, or maybe she was. But all he said was, "Uh-huh."

5

Bonnie came home for lunch/dinner on Monday, after her bi-weekly clean-up of an apartment in a divided-up old house in the village. Darcy was antsy for her to call Alberta, but Bonnie said, "It's barely nine o'clock there. You don't go making business calls first thing Monday morning unless it's an emergency, or unless you want to sound desperate." So they made up some tinned salmon salad for sandwiches, on the bread Melissa had helped them make yesterday. For all her business-cool, Bonnie didn't eat much, and tried not to watch the little hand crawl toward one. She held out till 1:10, then lifted the wall phone off its holder-charger.

The receptionist at the Wild Rose Credit Union accepted the charges immediately and patched her through to Sam Klassen, the contact name in the letter. Sam turned out to be Samantha, which probably gave Sam a one-up in assessing first contacts, depending on how the other person reacted to the surprise. After a few pleasant preliminaries, and establishing that they were still interested in interviewing Bonnie Marsden, and she in being interviewed, Bonnie said, "I'm afraid I wouldn't be able to fly out until sometime next week, and I'm not sure yet which day." A part of her noticed how easily she slipped back into white-collar ways of speaking, out of the no-collar she'd been wearing for a year and more.

Sam didn't even flinch at the fact that short notice lead time would make for a more expensive ticket. "Just let us know when you know, and we'll book the ticket. You'll be flying business class, of course."

Bonnie didn't say, *Of course.*

"I'm looking forward to meeting you, Bonnie."

"Oh, just one more thing. I'm curious . . . Would you mind telling me who forwarded you my résumé?"

"Certainly, I've got the papers right here. Oh yes, you came highly recommended by a gentleman named Bert Jackson."

"Bert Jackson?"

"He lives in Halifax, but does a lot of business with us. I assumed you knew him."

"I'm sure I do, just can't place him at the moment. Well, I'm looking forward to meeting you, too, Sam. Bye for now."

As Bonnie put the phone back on its cradle, Darcy said, "Wow, Mom. You didn't even jump up and down and scream."

"We haven't even signed a contract yet. *Then* I'll jump up and down and scream." She said it on automatic pilot; most of her was occupied in trying to place something. She muttered to herself, to see if hearing it aloud would help, "Bert Jackson . . . Bert Jackson . . ." A cold claw needled into the back of her neck. "Jack Burton."

Bonnie hefted the city phone book onto the table and opened it to the yellow pages. Ben had said *"an autobody shop in Dartmouth."* Dartmouth and Halifax were pretty much the same city, just on opposite sides of the harbour, but Dartmouthians could get very annoyed if you mistook them for Haligonians. The listing she was looking for didn't have a box ad, and wasn't bolded, but it had to be the right place.

Something told Bonnie to do what she was going to do before she had time to think about it. She reached down the phone again and dialled the number. After three rings, a recorded voice came on: "Burton's Body Shop. Everybody's busy working right now, so leave a message." Bonnie quickly switched off the phone and put it down, as though it had suddenly turned into dry ice in her hand. There was something in that voice that made her understand immediately why Ben had said, *"Jack Burton scared the bejesus out of me."* even when just one of a bunch of guys sitting around having a beer. Or rather, something *not* in that voice – any trace of any element another human being could contact. It wasn't a harsh or loud voice, and not exactly gravelly, more like it was filtering through sand. Not exactly whispering, but not making any effort to make itself heard, because you better make an effort to listen. And she didn't think she was imagining that the voice salted a twisted, self-contained sense of humour into 'body shop.'

The sound of the voice made her almost see someone who fit the voice perfectly, but Bonnie couldn't quite get the image into focus. It was a movie actor who was tall, dark and not exactly handsome. Not as big as Clint Eastwood, but scarier. Not as wild as Jack Palance, but more evil. But, no . . . thinking of "scary" and "evil" was what was throwing her off. Those concepts didn't exist in the world of this actor's characters. He was simply someone going about his business, who would prefer not to meet any obstacles along the way, but if you made yourself an obstacle . . . Obstacles unfortunately had to be removed. And the actor was . . . Henry Silva.

Bonnie's hands clasped themselves together for warmth, seeing the image that the voice on that answering machine had conjured up. Henry Silva hadn't made a lot of Hollywood movies, but he'd stuck in her mind like barbed glass. And not just hers. A while back, Bonnie had been tea-chatting in one of her customer's kitchens, and had found herself nattering on about some article she'd read in the Entertainment section, something she tended to fall into when there was nothing real to talk about. In this case, an article on a new movie Henry Silva had suddenly reappeared in had explained why he'd disappeared from Hollywood movies for years: back when, he'd been hired to do a movie in Italy and discovered he had an amazing knack for learning languages. So for years he'd been starring in Italian movies, French movies, Portugese movies, German movies . . . In mid-prattle,

Bonnie had cut herself off, and apologized for being so foolish as to chatter about obscure, old movie actors no one else would remember. The other person had said, "Oh, no – you see that face once, you never forget it." At first glimpse, it looked like a face wearing a mask, but once you saw the eyes, it looked like a mask wearing a face.

Now that old movies had given Bonnie an image she could fit to the voice, she could clearly see a new movie, of what had happened on that backwoods road one night last week.

A rusty, little car grinds to a halt at an old, logging road turn-off and switches off its headlights. The driver, window rolled down, is blonde-haired, skinny-faced, thick-spectacled Billy Vickers, bopping along to some stoned-out soundtrack in his head. Out of the dark woods comes a tall, black figure: black gloves and clothes, black hair and black-mirror eyes. Whether the clothes are a silk suit or an old sweater and workpants, there is always a kind of panther elegance to the man. He is carrying a light of some sort . . .

The picture stalled there, on what kind of light he would be carrying. It would have to be some kind of kerosene or propane lantern. Right, an old style hurricane lamp, basically just a wire frame around a glass chimney and reservoir, all of which would melt away in a car fire.

Jack Burton walks quickly toward the car, not giving Billy a pause to think of climbing out, saying, "Hello, Billy. Glad you got my message . . ."

"Hi, Jack." Billy giggles at his accidental joke. "What's with the hurricane lamp? Can't afford a flashlight?"

Jack Burton continues his walk toward the car, and continues his sentence, ". . . but you didn't get all *my message, yet. C.O.D., kid."*

The hurricane lamp flies through the air to smash against the driver's door and gush flame. As Billy Vickers screams, Jack Burton steps back to be out of range when the gas tank explodes. Jack Burton says pleasantly, "Glad to see you were wearing your seat belt. Safety first."

"Mom?" Bonnie blinked her way back into her kitchen. Darcy was saying, "Are you all right? Where did you go?"

"Oh, I just . . . You know sometimes when you make a phone call and you get an answering machine when you expected a person, and you suddenly can't remember what you were going to say and your brain goes Tilt?"

"Yeah, sure, Mom." But she sounded a bit doubtful.

"Anyway, I remembered now." Bonnie picked up the phone again and pressed Redial. She consciously shut out listening to the voice on the answering machine, just listened for the beep, then said, "Hello, this is Bonnie Marsden. I . . . think there's something I should thank you for," and left her number.

Darcy volunteered to meet Melissa at the school bus and take her for a walk in the woods, since it'd be Darcy's last chance before going back to the city tomorrow. Bonnie busied herself with things around the house, like setting out clean sheets to put on her bed tomorrow, when it would be her and Ben's bed again. She tried to keep her imagination from chasing what possible reason Jack Burton might've had for 'highly recommending' her to the Wild Rose Credit Union, since she probably couldn't imagine it anyway. Darcy and Melissa came back from the woods flush-cheeked and famished, and chowed down on pork chops from the half a pig Ben had got in trade for some odd job.

After supper clean-up and a bit of TV, Darcy took charge of Melissa's bathtime and bedtime, while Bonnie sat in the kitchen and smoked a cigarette, her seventh or eighth of the day. For years she'd been holding herself to four or five, and some days even less. But her nerves were wound tight enough already without allowing herself a little slack. Over the last six weeks, it would've been more than easy to slide back into a pack a day, but if Ben could go cold turkey with his addiction, the least she could do was hold hers near its baseline. It took some effort, though, at times, and today her nerves had got wound a notch or two tighter. She looked at the clock. Business hours at Burton's Autobody must be over by now, if not long over. And still no reply to the message she'd left. Maybe there wouldn't be one. Maybe she'd never know why someone who was 'smart and tough and crazy' had decided to do her a favour. That didn't feel very comfortable.

Darcy came down the hall from Melissa's bedroom, brandishing the purple plastic pen she'd probably had to arm-wrestle Melissa to get away from her. "Melissa's even harder to get to bed than I was!"

"Don't bet on it."

"Well, it's getting easier as I get older."

"Darcy!"

Darcy laughed. "Not *that* easy."

The phone rang.

Bonnie straightened her shoulders and took a deep breath before picking it up. "Hello?"

That voice said, "Bonnie Marsden." It wasn't a question, or a request, just a statement.

Bonnie endeavoured to keep her voice relatively normal, reminding herself that there were miles of phone line between her and the man at the other end. "Mr. Burton. Or should I say Mr. Jackson?"

"There's no Mr. Jackson works here. Somebody's misinformed you." Bonnie was sure she heard a slight twist on 'informed.'

"Maybe, but I'm dead sure it was you that got my résumé to that credit union in Alberta. I just don't know why."

"I don't much like telephone conversations. But I'll be passing through Membertou County tomorrow night, got some business to take care of. I could meet you at nine o'clock, dead end of MacGuigan Road. You know where?"

"Sure, used to be MacGuigans' Sawmill. But . . . Ben's getting out tomorrow."

"I won't interrupt your party for long. If you don't show, you don't show. But, no more phone calls." Click.

As Bonnie put the phone back in its cradle, a bit shakily, Darcy said, "Mom . . . isn't Jack Burton the name you said gave Dad the chills?"

"Your father doesn't have to know about it. I'm just going to ask the man a simple question that isn't a threat to him in any way. If he didn't want to answer it, he wouldn't've arranged to meet me." Bonnie wondered whether she was reassuring Darcy or herself. "Anyway, he's got no reason to be antsy around some middle-aged, hick cleaning lady."

They played a rubber of cribbage, and Darcy yawned her way through the third game, mispegging several times. Bonnie said, "I think you're not used to hiking around in country air. You don't have to sit up with me. I'm like a Christmas Eve kid. No need for both of us to be bleary in the morning."

Darcy got up and kissed her on the cheek and sleepwalked down the hallway to her room. "Christmas Eve" reminded Bonnie that there was a tail end of Bailey's Irish Cream in the cupboard, left over from last Christmas. She poured a little into her tea and sat smoking another cigarette, looking across the table at the purple, green and orange pen-recorder.

She remembered an odd thing in the news a while back. A couple of undercover Boston police officers had lured some Boston gangster up to Halifax, pretending they were trying to set up a smuggling operation. The reason they'd wanted to talk to him in Halifax, was that he'd always covered his tracks so well they couldn't get a judge to sign off on a wiretap sanction. But under Nova Scotia law, any conversation recorded by anybody can be used as evidence, as long as one person in the conversation knows it's being recorded. Or maybe it was Canadian law all across the board, all across the border. That question popped into Bonnie's mind and she popped it right out again. All that mattered was that, according to her 'jackdaw memory,' that was the law in Nova Scotia, which included the dead end of MacGuigan Road.

Bonnie picked up the pen, found the tiny Record switch hidden in one of the orange swirls, said a few words, then found the Playback switch hidden in one of the neon green swirls. It didn't sound much like her. But then, everybody's recorded voice sounds different to them. Melissa's voice on playback had sounded much like Melissa to Bonnie, just reduced in volume through that microscopic speaker-thingy or whatever it was inside there. Jack Burton had one of those dry, self-contained voices that would reproduce even more like the original. His voice on the answering machine hadn't sounded all that much different from when he was talking through the phone in person.

Bonnie held the pen out straight-armed in front of her, flicked the Record button and said a few words. It played back just fine. Not that her arm's length was all that long, but about as far as people stood from each other in a normal conversation. She took down the notepad from beside the phone and practised writing and turning the recorder on at the same time. After a few tries, she found a hand position where she could print legibly and click the switch on with just a tiny flick of her thumb. She poured herself another cup of Irish tea and kept on practising. The Mounties couldn't catch Jack Burton, Federal Excise couldn't catch him; what was going to catch him was a ten-dollar kid's toy. She hoped.

Early afternoon the next day found Bonnie sitting in her aged Honda in the Correctional Facility's parking lot, looking at the candy apple red and concrete grey sprawl of a building, some of it one storey, some of it much taller. She sat there long enough to get antsy, then got out and walked around the car a few times. Men began to come out of the institute's front door, some carrying plastic bags, some with bookbag-style knapsacks slung over one shoulder. They emerged one at a time from between the two red pillars that held a red steel awning above the entranceway. Some of the men were met by friends or family, some climbed into waiting cabs, some walked alone toward the nearest bus stop. Finally, one came out who was taller and wider than any of the others.

Bonnie ran across the parking lot and didn't quite knock Ben off his feet when she hurled herself against him. They stood pressed together and rocking from side to side for a moment, then Ben stepped back and gazed around and upward. He said, "Look at all that sky."

Bonnie crooked her arm around his to walk him to the car. Ben said concernedly, "You're looking tired. I mean, you're looking damn good, but tired."

"I didn't get much sleep last night."

"Know what you mean. But that's the last night."

"Darcy wanted to sit up with me, but there was no point in two of us being bleary. I dropped her off on the way here. I told her she could come along and welcome you out, but she said we probably wouldn't need company just now."

"Smart girl."

"But she asked me to get you to call her at work once we get home. So she'll know for sure you're out, and there wasn't some last-minute screw-up. Would you like a beer?"

"Huh?"

Bonnie opened the hatchback and pulled back the polar fleece blanket that lived in there, showing three cans of Keith's nestled on a plastic bag of ice cubes. Ben said, "Right out here in the parking lot?" She produced a plastic sleeve with a ginger ale label on it, a relic of Moyle's high school days. "Funny, two months ago I wouldn't've thought twice about it. But, don't we have to get going so we're there for Melissa's school bus?"

"She's going to Cindy's after school. I told her we'd pick her up for supper."

"That was good thinking." He popped the can and took a healthy swallow. "Man, that tastes good." He took another, then said, "You know, I didn't want to say anything while I was in there, just worry you, but now's I'm out . . . People bitch about prisoners getting cable TV and free nicotine patches and all those goodies when they're supposed to be being punished. Maybe it makes a difference to some guys, but me, I don't care how many colour TVs they put in there, there's still locks on the doors and I ain't got a key." He took another swallow, then extended the can. "Want a slurp?"

"Sure." Bonnie took a small sip, handed the can back and decided now was as good a time as any. "Oh, I'm afraid I'll have to go out for a little while tonight, around nine o'clock. There's somebody in the village who works evenings and wants me to look over her place and give an estimate. Could be a steady customer. Seems kind of foolish, since I'll probably be out of the cleaning-lady business in a couple of weeks, but 'probably' isn't for sure."

Ben didn't say anything to that, just upended the can over his mouth and said, "Well, that one's a dead pumpkin. Let's go *home*."

As they climbed into the car, Bonnie said, "Oh, I left your cousin in the tape deck."

"Huh?" She pushed the button and the music came on. "Oh, yeah, Cousin Gerry."

Unfortunately, what Gerry Marsden came out singing was:
Chills, running up and down my spine,
Woh, I get them every time,
Woh-oh-oh, I got chills . . .

Once Bonnie had pulled her car in beside Ben's truck and switched off the engine, they raced each other to the bedroom. Bonnie took the sneaky way, through the back basement door, and got there first. An hour or so later, Ben murmured, "Guess we better be thinking of getting dressed and going to get Melissa." Up in the kitchen, buttoning his last buttons, he said, "Amazing. My own shirt. Smells like fresh air, 'stead of the prison laundry. Fits me, too."

He popped another can of Keith's – only his third in three hours, and he hadn't pulled out the bottle beside them in the fridge – and stood looking out the kitchen window at the backyard and gardens he'd worked so hard on over the years. He said, without turning away from the window, "Alcohol . . . alcoholics . . . I talked to a couple counsellors while I was in there . . ."

Now he turned from the window to face Bonnie at the kitchen table and waved his hand as though brushing something away. "Oh, I don't mean I'm gonna go all A.A. on you or anything. Fat chance. What I was getting from them counsellors was information. It's amazing how ignorant most people are, or at least *I* was, about alcohol, even if they been drinking it for thirty years. Like, if you get just mildly hammered one night, sleep for eight hours, get up feeling fine, chances are there's still enough alcohol in your bloodstream to make you legally impaired."

"You're kidding." Bonnie thought of how many mornings

she might've been driving to work feeling perfectly fine, but if she'd got in an accident and got breathalyzed she would've been blamed, even if it were the other driver's fault. And she would've blamed herself.

"Nope. Just scientific fact. After you've been up and moving for a few hours, you'll be below the impaired line. But if you have a beer with your dinner, you're not just having that beer, it's ganging up with whatever's still left in you from the night before. And then the other thing is tolerance."

Bonnie thought of making a crack about already being as tolerant as any wife could be, but decided not.

"Your body's tolerance for alcohol just keeps getting bigger the more you keep feeding it. One of the counsellors told me he knew a guy who seemed perfectly normal when he had three times the legal limit in him. Now, my tolerance never got near that bad, but I'm sure it got bigger than it was ten years ago. Well, now I got a chance to start from scratch. The trick is keeping track, not let it creep up on you. I thought of a couple ways to do that. I'll try 'em out and see what works."

Ben took another sip of his beer, then shrugged. "So I'm an addict, so what? Lots of people are addicted to caffeine."

Bonnie said, "But that doesn't hurt anybody else," and then thought of the number of times she'd seen people being nasty and hasty just because they'd had too much caffeine, or not enough.

"You said yourself you haven't seen me falling-down drunk in years. Oh, I was supposed to phone Darcy . . ."

Bonnie sat smoking her third cigarette of the day and half-listening to Ben's half of the phone conversation. After he'd basically explained that he was truly free and clear again, there was a longish pause, as though Darcy was going on about something. But he didn't chuckle or react in any other lively way to Darcy's usually very lively going-on, just said flatly, "Huh," and then "Where'd you say?" After another bit of a pause, he said, "No, that's okay. See you soon. Thanks for calling. Oh, I called you, didn't I? Well, bye for now."

After Ben hung up, Bonnie said, "What was where?"

"Huh?"

"You said, 'Where'd you say?'."

"Oh, that was a . . . friend of Darcy's had been telling her about a cheaper apartment, but maybe in a rough neighbourhood. I told her it's okay, right on the edge of a helluva rough neighbourhood, but not in it. We better get going before Melissa thinks we forgot her."

Ben wanted them to go in his truck, to give it a run after sitting so long. Bonnie couldn't see why that couldn't wait until tomorrow, but he insisted. So she had to sit in the truck drumming her fingers for a few minutes while he coaxed and cursed it into starting. He seemed relieved when it smoothed out from coughing and sputtering once they got down to the stop sign at the bottom of the hill. But he insisted on a slight detour to get ten bucks of gas, saying, "What's in here's lost all its octane, needs a goose. I guess we're all better off having everything unleaded now, but it sure goes sour fast."

Melissa came tearing out of her friend's house like a rocket aimed at her father. On the drive home, Bonnie had to keep an eye on her to make sure she didn't clutch at Ben's arm while he was trying to shift gears. Bonnie had splurged on two steaks for supper, one for Ben and one for her and Melissa. As it was, Bonnie had to work at choking down even half of her half. Nine o'clock kept looming up and constricting her throat.

Ben said around his first mouthful, "Ain't that wonderful. Food that tastes like food."

Melissa said, "Din't they have a good cook where you 'uz working?"

"No, they surely did not."

Despite enjoying his eating, Ben seemed a bit distracted. Bonnie figured it was only natural, after six weeks of living in another world, that it would take him a while to get adjusted to this one again. After supper, Ben headed downstairs to get his reading glasses for the paper, and Clyde followed him. After being brought in off the line to wolf down his supper, Clyde had waited patiently while the family ate theirs and gave him a dessert-snack of leftovers. But now he wasn't going to let Ben out of his sight.

Melissa started helping Bonnie clear the table, then suddenly stopped and wailed, "Oh no!"

"What's wrong, honey?"

"I left something at Cindy's!"

It flashed through Bonnie's mind that 'something' might be the pen-recorder, which would pretty much bury her clever-crazy plan to catch Jack Burton. Part of her was relieved that she might not have to go through with it. "What'd you leave there?"

"My gold hair-thing!"

The hair clip wasn't actually gold, of course, just gold-coloured plastic. But it was precious to Melissa, in the same way Ben's vintage John Deere cap was precious to him. "Well, you can just phone Cindy and ask her to bring it to school tomorrow. I've got the number here." Bonnie reached down the phone for Melissa, and peeled off the notepad sheet where she'd written down Cindy's family's number in case the plans to pick up Melissa got convoluted. "Do you remember where the talk button is?"

"Uh-huh." Melissa beeped the Talk button and two-handed the phone up to her ear. After a few seconds she lowered the phone again and beeped the Talk button off.

"What's the matter, dear? My numbers hard to read?"

"Daddy's on the phone. With some lady."

"Oh. Well, I'm sure he'll be off in a couple of minutes."

A couple of minutes later, Clyde came prancing up the stairs with Ben lumbering behind him. Ben seemed a touch taken aback to see Melissa with the phone. As Melissa proceeded with her phone call, Bonnie said to Ben, "Who were you talking to?"

"Oh, Paul Nextdoor wanted me to call when I was out for sure. Same as Darcy, but for different reasons. He's got some work lined up for me. Paul wasn't there so I left the message with Elsie."

Ben sat down with his newspaper – yesterday's newspaper, since the old fella across the road let them have his when he was done with them, which saved them almost twenty dollars a month. Melissa proudly finished her telephone adventure and handed the phone to Bonnie to hang up. Then Melissa fished the purple plastic pen out of her pint-sized backpack, crawled up between her father and his newspaper and proceeded to demonstrate. Eventually Melissa wound down and fell asleep on Ben's lap. Clyde curled up beside their chair and snuffled his way into doggy dreamland. Bonnie could understand both dog and daughter. Home was home again.

After awhile, Ben said softly across the table, indicating the top of Melissa's head with his chin, "Uh . . ."

Bonnie said, also softly, "She hasn't been sleeping well the last six weeks. I think we can skip bath time for one night."

"Okay." Ben stood up with Melissa in his arms and carried her down the hall toward her bedroom. Bonnie poured herself another cup of tea and smoked another cigarette. The plastic cigarette case that had come with the rolling kit was half empty, and it was only Tuesday. Usually, what she rolled on Sunday evening would last her the week. On impulse, she poured the last of the bottle of Irish Cream into her tea, hoping it might steady her nerves.

Ben came back carrying the pen, saying, "Even half asleep I had to pry it out of her hand. Said it was the bestest birthday present ever. I sure am one smart shopper." He put the pen on the table and picked up his newspaper again.

It seemed to Bonnie that by rights they should be talking about Alberta, making plans for what would be the best day next week to fly out there, and who would be the best to leave Melissa with for a few schooldays. But there wasn't much point in starting a long conversation that would just get cut off when she had to leave for MacGuigan Road. Besides, her mind wasn't really on Alberta at the moment. It was on how to get the pen off the table and into her pocket without Ben wondering why she had to take Melissa's pen to her appointment, instead of the several in the notepad holder beside the phone.

At eight-thirty, Bonnie put her purse on the table and ostentatiously rummaged and rattled through it. "Damn, I've lost my keys again."

Ben looked at her over the rims of his reading glasses and his newspaper. "On the hook?"

Bonnie went to the front door hallway, where a little row of keyhooks hung beside the coathooks, although she knew her key ring wasn't hanging there. She came back saying, "Nope, not there."

"Well, you've got a spare, don't you? Or you can use my car key."

"Yeah, but I still gotta find my keys. There's some on there for houses I clean." She made a show of digging through her purse again, and came out with them. "There, the sidepocket I never use." She clanked the keys down on the table beside the pen. She left them there, went back to the front hall to get her not-quite-winter coat and came back into the kitchen, saying, "Honestly, I'd lose my head if it wasn't screwed-on. Or screwed-up." She scooped up the keys and the pen at the same time, tucked them quickly in her pocket and headed for the door. "I don't think this'll take long."

"Come home safe."

6

The mouth of MacGuigan Road wasn't all that far from Piziquid Village in miles, but Bonnie had to take a Z-shaped route to get there on pavement. She slowed down as she turned onto the gravel. Barely gravel – the road didn't get much use or upkeep since the MacGuigans shut down the sawmill and sold off the machinery. About a quarter mile in, the road came to an end in a clearing around a bulldozed heap of old buildings. Bonnie switched off the ignition, but left the electrics on for the park lights. She flicked the dome light switch to stay on when the doors were closed, then got out quickly and stepped away from the car. There was no sound but the faint tapping and whispering of branches in the overhead breeze. The ground was thick with autumn leaves, but still sodden from the last rain, so they didn't crackle or rustle.

That voice came out of the darkness: "So you're Bonnie Marsden." Bonnie's head snapped around in that direction. The man who stepped into the light wasn't tall and dark, and there was nothing remotely elegant about him. He wasn't exactly short or tall, not exactly thin or fat, and mostly grey: a grey, canvassy sort-of parka jacket, hanging open over a sweatshirt of indeterminate colour, greyish beard and longish hair that blended in the back with the fur trim on the hood of his coat, greyish-white complexion, and greyish-blue eyes behind wire-rimmed glasses.

That was the most unexpected part of all. Jack Burton was supposed to be a tough guy, and tough guys weren't supposed to wear glasses. Not that tough guys couldn't have weak eyes, but wearing glasses could lose you an eye if you got sucker-punched. Then Bonnie realized that it made perfect sense that Jack Burton would wear glasses. He was never the one who got sucker-punched.

Bonnie said, trying to make her voice come out casual through her fluttering throat, "So you're Jack Burton. Or should I say Bert Jackson?"

He gave out a little half-cough that might've been his version of a laugh. "Yeah, I heard you were pretty good at sussing things out. Bert Jackson's got his own phone line. I don't much like telephones, but out here . . ." He arced one arm out to indicate the dark clearing and the woods, "I can say anything I want. I know you're not wearing a wire."

"How would you know that?"

"I know you're cozy with Corporal Kowalchuck, so I sussed out whether there's been a requisition for a wire through the Membertou County RCMP. Don't ask me how."

"I won't. But . . . how did you get my résumé?"

"Oh, I know some people that know some people, and it wasn't hard to guess where around here you would've sent your résumé. Then it was just a question of getting it copied and sending it out to Alberta, along with a nice note from the nice Mr. Jackson who pumps a lot of nice money through the Wild Rose Credit Union."

"But . . . *why?* Why would you send my résumé out to Alberta?"

"Your husband's a stand-up guy, Bonnie Marsden. All he had to do was say a few words when the cops mentioned my name, and he wouldn't have pulled time on that chickenshit charge. And if the cops had had even a little bit of back-up for what they heard from that little shit –"

"Billy Vickers."

"That's right – my lawyers would've found it harder to say

the case against me was a joke. And once they got you on one charge, the ratting starts to work its way up the line. The domino effect, you know. Ben stopped it, this time. But you've got a terrible reputation for being nosy, and I figured you and Ben were bound to talk from time to time, so . . ."

"So you figured on helping us out . . . of town."

There was that little cough again. "I wouldn't want Ben's wife to become a problem."

"Well, I guess I'm gonna feel safer in Alberta than here. But, um, they're bound to expect me to know at least a little about Bert Jackson."

"Tell 'em he's your second cousin or something. He's in the auto business, too. Imports used cars from out west where they don't salt the roads. Jackson's Auto Auctions."

"I'll just write that on my hand." Bonnie pretended to rummage in her coat pockets, and came out with the purple plastic pen. She made an attempt at a realistic-sounding chuckle. "You know you've been a mother too long when you start stealing your kids' school pens." While printing Jackson's Auto Auctions on the palm of her left hand, ridiculously wondering whether the pen would write through sweat, Bonnie said, "You killed the little shit, didn't you?" and flicked the Record switch with a twitch of her thumb.

"Billy Vickers?" This time the sound was definitely a laugh. "Hell, I *flambéd* the little bastard." Then Jack Burton's voice abruptly changed. "What'd you just do?"

"Nothing, I just –"

"Gimme the pen."

"No, I just –"

His hand shot out to trap her wrist in a vice grip. "Gimme the pen or I'll rip your hand off!"

The vice grip began to twist. There was no breaking free of it, and no use hitting at Jack Burton with her other hand. And once he'd got his hands on the pen, he'd figure it out soon enough. She looked up at the grey and white face, to see if she'd have any hope of convincing him that she'd made a mistake and would never do it again. There was nothing there but stone and ice. It was likely to be the last thing she would ever see. *And all because I had to be so goddamn clever.*

Two huge, open hands appeared behind Jack Burton's neck and closed around it. The grip on Bonnie's wrist was gone, as Jack Burton's hands flailed back at the ones wrapped around his neck and throat. The light from the car went just far enough that Bonnie could make out, above and behind Jack Burton's head, the half-shadowed face of Big Ben Marsden. Ben's lips were pulled back from his teeth, but not in a snarl, more like in concentration.

Jack Burton gave up grappling at Ben's hands, and tried to punch and kick backward at his body and legs. But Ben's arms held straight out made it too long a reach. The flailing was getting jerkier and weaker. Jack Burton's right hand fumbled at his coat pocket, trying to reach inside. Bonnie batted the hand away. It started to come back, but then went limp, as did the rest of Jack Burton's body, the badger-grey head lolling forward from Ben's hands. Ben lowered him face down on the ground, then crouched beside him and looked around frantically, as though trying to find something or think of something. Bonnie could see the light bulb go on over Ben's head as he whipped off his belt and started to bind Jack Burton's wrists together behind his back.

Bonnie gasped out, "Where did you . . . ? How did you . . .?"

"Oh, Darcy told me, that's why she wanted me to call her at work." Ben hurried on with tightening and knotting the belt, as though he didn't expect Jack Burton to be out for long. "There's a straight way from our place to here, on a backroad that would've took the bottom off your car, comes out on t'other side of this little ravine. If this hadn't turned ugly, I would've left here when you did, and you'd never've knowed."

"Ben, he was trying to reach something in his coat pocket, maybe a gun . . .?"

"Well, he can't reach it now." Ben stood up. "What's on the pen?"

"What?"

"Bonnie, if there's nothing on that pen, it's just our word against his, of what he said and what we heard. He could end up walking around free, knowing you tried to trap him and I jumped him from behind. He knows where we live."

Bonnie realized that she'd dropped the pen when she'd batted Jack Burton's hand away from his coat pocket. She peered around, hoping to God she hadn't stepped on it. She saw a swatch of bright colour in a nest of brown leaves, picked up the pen and clicked the playback button. Jack Burton's voice came out loud and clear: *"Billy Vickers? Hell, I flambéd the little bastard!"*

Ben laughed, seemingly mostly from relief. "Bonnie, you're still the craziest damn woman I ever met, but I'd say you got the sonuvabitch. You got your cell phone in the car?"

"Yeah." The cell phone was an extra expense, but with Bonnie working at so many different places, and sometimes needing to call a new place for directions, and Melissa's school needing a reliable number just in case . . . Anyway, they didn't put many calls on it.

"Well, you go call 911 and I'll keep an eye on him. That belt ain't exactly a scientific restraint."

When Bonnie got back from the car, Jack Burton appeared to've come to. His eyes were open and his breathing was no longer sleep-like slow and deep. But he wasn't moving or saying anything, just lying there with his hands behind his back and his head pillowed sideways on the leaves. Somehow, his stillness was more nervous-making than if he'd been cursing and trying to break free.

Ben looked up from where he'd crouched down again to keep a close eye. "They coming?"

"Yeah. Should be soon." Bonnie nodded down toward the on-lighted cell phone in her hand. "The dispatcher wants me to stay on the line till they get here."

Ben nodded back, then said, "Oh, about Melissa, no need to worry. When I called Paul Nextdoor and he wasn't there . . . ? I was actually calling Elsie to see if her or one of their teenagers would come over and watch our TV for awhile, in case Melissa wakes up."

"Good. Ben?"

"Yeah?"

There was a question Bonnie very much wanted to ask him, but realized it wasn't something she should ask while Jack Burton or anybody else was there to hear it. Including the dispatcher listening in on what came through the cell phone. "No, it's okay, not important, I'll ask you later."

In not very long, Bonnie heard a siren, and then saw red and blue lights flaring through the trees as a police car came tearing down MacGuigan Road as fast as it dared tear. She said into the cell phone, "They're here," and clicked it off.

It turned out to be two Mountie cars. Out of the first one stepped Corporal Kowalchuck, and out of the second the young, new, black Constable States. Not new to Membertou County, he'd grown up in East Raddallton, where black families had been living for two hundred years. Two of his uncles used to play on the same junior hockey team as Ben.

Bonnie stepped away from Ben and Jack Burton to intercept Corporal Kowalchuck. She explained what had happened as quickly as possible, and played what the pen had recorded. Corporal Kowalchuck just shook his head slowly, murmured, "I don't know why they bother paying me," and took a plastic evidence bag out of his jacket pocket. Bonnie dropped the pen in and he handed it to the constable.

Ben stood up as Bonnie and the Mounties approached. Bonnie said to Corporal Kowalchuck, "He was trying to reach something out of his right-hand coat pocket, while Ben was – I mean, before he passed out."

Corporal Kowalchuck took out a pair of surgical gloves and pulled one onto his right hand, in the standard practice of pointing his hand upward with the fingers splayed. Then he let the wrist elastic snap to, and looked down at Jack Burton lying there with his backside upside. Jack Burton said the only two words he'd spoken since Ben grabbed him. "Very funny."

Corporal Kowalchuck crouched down, reached into the pocket and came out with what Bonnie'd expected, but not exactly what she'd expected. It was a gun, but not the kind of flat little automatic Bonnie'd thought a modern gangster would carry in his pocket. It was a snub-nosed revolver, the barrel almost as wide as it was long.

Corporal Kowalchuck seemed a bit surprised, too, as much as he was likely to register surprise. He said, "Huh. This is almost an antique. But you're quite right, Mr. Burton, they don't make 'em like they used to. And a pocket revolver won't jam up on you like a pistol might."

Jack Burton said nothing.

Corporal Kowalchuck placed the pocket revolver in the evidence bag the constable held out, then said, "Lucky for you, Ben, he reacted instinctively. Lucky for both of you."

"Damn right."

Bonnie was about to ask what that meant, then realized. The natural human reaction was first to try and pry the hands off your throat. By the time Jack Burton got past that to thinking of his pocket gun, it had been too late. It was strange to think there might be anything natural or human about Jack Burton, and a little discomforting.

Corporal Kowalchuck took out his handcuffs, looked down at Jack Burton's belt-bound-hands and said, "Sorry, Ben, I'm afraid we'll have to hold your belt as evidence. His lawyer's bound to want to see it."

"That's okay, I got another one at home. That one's getting too tight anyways."

"We'll take care of Mr. Burton from here. You two might as well go home, and come into the detachment sometime tomorrow to give your statements. But, uh, for now, I . . . really don't know what to say to you two – give you a lecture or give you a medal."

Ben said, "You already gave us a medal – told us we could go home."

By the time Bonnie got home, Ben's truck was already there.

Ben was sitting in the kitchen with a tall glass of clear liquid that certainly wasn't all water and ice cubes. Ben said, "Elsie Nextdoor's gone back next door. Said Melissa didn't make a peep."

Bonnie thought of sitting down, but wasn't sure she'd be able to get up again. She said, "I thought I'd be wired, but I can hardly keep my eyes open. Guess I came down on the drive home."

"Yeah, I know what you mean. Why don't you go on down and get snuggled in. I'll go give Clyde a walk around the yard and bring him in."

"Okay. See you in a minute."

"Yeah."

Bonnie got herself downstairs and out of her clothes and into her nightgown and into bed, and a minute later heard music. She looked at the clock. It wasn't a minute later, it was two o'clock in the morning. The music was coming from the rec room across the hall, and it was definitely 'Cousin Gerry,' although she couldn't tell which song he was singing. She got up and drew on her two-Christmases-ago dressing gown. When she opened the bedroom door, she could hear that the song was the one Gerry Marsden had written about turning his back on Swinging London to go home to Liverpool:

People around every corner, they seem to smile and say,
"We don't care what your name is, boy, we'll never turn you away."
So ferry 'cross the Mersey, 'cause this land's the place I love,
And here I'll stay . . .

Bonnie paused outside the bedroom doorway to look into the rec room. Ben was sitting back in his well-worn La-Z-Boy, with his drink in his hand, chewing on his lower lip. His head jerked around when she stepped into the light, and he moved to straighten his chair up so he could reach the stereo knobs. "Sorry, Bonnie, I didn't know it was that loud –"

"It isn't. I just sort of drifted half awake and you weren't there, no different from the last six weeks, and then I remembered it *was* different, but you still weren't there."

"Oh, sorry, I, uh, I could tell I wasn't gonna nod off right off, so . . . I guess my body's so happy it's not in a cage anymore, it doesn't want me to fall asleep and miss anything."

She waited for him to say more. When he didn't, she went and perched on the edge of the couch nearest his chair. She said, "That isn't it, is it?"

"No." He took a sip of his drink, held it in his mouth a moment, then swallowed. "Alberta. I didn't want to say anything about it, 'cause it sounded so selfish, but . . . You haven't had much chance to think about it, and I ain't had nothing to do but sit around and think about things –"

"That and knock out psycho murderers."

"Yeah, well, that was . . ." Ben half-flapped one hand to brush that away. "We got a *home* here, Bonnie. My great-grandfather left the capital of Ireland 'cause it was the only way he could survive. If the only way we could survive here was go on welfare or something, I'd say hell yes, let's move to Alberta or Timbuktu or wherever we can make a living. But, the fact is, we're getting by."

This was coming at Bonnie out of nowhere, and she realized it shouldn't have. It seemed to her that if anyone had been sounding selfish lately, it wasn't Ben. She said, "You're right that I haven't had much chance to stop and think about things. But, there's gotta be more than just getting by."

"There is. There's this rundown old bungalow that you and me bust our butts turning into a decent house for kids to grow up in. There's the garden that was just cooch-grass when we moved in, and now whenever Robbie or Darcy come to visit we're sending them home with bags of organic carrots and potatoes and whatever. There's the trout pond out back that used to be a swamp. There's the people you see in the hardware store, and you know who they are and they know who you are, but nobody messes in anybody else's business unless there's trouble. There's a lot more than just getting by."

Bonnie could feel the gift of her new future slipping out of her hands, but that wasn't all she was feeling. "Ben, why did you go to jail instead of paying the fine?"

"You know that as well as I do. If we started carrying a loan to pay the fine, pretty soon we'd be missing a mortgage payment here and there, and next thing you know the bank'd be taking this place away from us, and where're we gonna go?"

"If you could spend six weeks in a cage so we can keep on living here, the least I can do is pass up a chance to wear business clothes again."

"But, you'd be giving up a secure job."

"There's nothing secure anymore, Ben." She reached out and put her hand on his forearm on his chairarm. "Almost."

Ben looked down at her hand, and his mouth scrunched up like he didn't know what to say. She was going to say, *Maybe we can both sleep now,* and get up. But there was that question she'd started to ask him back on MacGuigan Road, and then cut herself off because she couldn't ask the question when there was anybody else around to hear the answer. "Ben?"

"Hm?"

"What would've happened if the pen hadn't caught what Jack Burton said?"

He shrugged. "Like I said, there'd be a good chance he'd end up roaming around free, and he knows where we live."

"So, if when you asked me to play it back, it hadn't played back him admitting he killed Billy Vickers, then what?"

Ben laughed, but it sounded like a diversionary laugh. "'Then what?' is exactly what I was asking myself. I dunno, Bonnie. The pen *did* catch him. Who knows what would've happened if it didn't? I dunno 'then what,' or 'what if,' 'cause the 'then' and the 'if' never happened."

"But . . . you were so antsy to hear what was on the pen immediately, the instant you had Jack Burton tied up. Like you had to make a fast decision. Like if what he said hadn't been recorded, you already had some idea of 'what then.'"

Ben looked at her from the longest distance ever in all their lives together, and said flatly, "Then I'd've told you to get in your car and go home."

Mid-morning, Bonnie and Ben drove in to the RCMP station to give their statements. Constable States took Ben into a side room to take his statement; Bonnie gave hers in Corporal Kowalchuck's cubbyhole of an office. When Corporal Kowalchuck had finished with his "just the facts, ma'am," he said, "There's a development this morning you should find reassuring. You re-member I said that if my detachment was the one that finally put a case together against Jack Burton, I'd be sleeping with a shotgun beside my bed?"

"Yeah." That didn't sound particularly reassuring.

"Well, I won't be. Mr. Burton decided, through his very expensive lawyer, to forego bail. It's a highly unusual decision, especially for someone with financial resources. I wouldn't presume to be able to understand Mr. Burton's trains of thought, and I don't think I'd like to be able to, but I think at least part of the reason for *this* decision, was insurance."

"Insurance?"

"In case anything should happen to you, or your husband, or to me or anybody else involved in this case. Suspicion would naturally fall in Mr. Burton's direction, especially since the charge against him is the murder of a potential Crown witness. But, you see, one of the reasons it's been very difficult to pin anything on him is, Jack Burton does his own dirty work. No hired enforcers, no accomplices. So you can rest assured that as long as Jack Burton is in jail, any 'accident' that might befall you or your husband will be an accident." Corporal Kowalchuck smiled pleasantly. "Unless, of course, you have other enemies of a murderous bent."

7

Jack Burton's actual trial didn't happen for months, what with preliminary hearings and discoveries and motions to postpone and Crown Disclosures and what-not. None of which required Bonnie or Ben's participation; they were free to carry on their lives as if they'd never met Jack Burton. Christmas came and went, and with it Darcy and Robbie and even Moyle, all the way from north Alberta for a whole week. Moyle and his father hardly argued at all. The snow came and stayed. Most winters in Nova Scotia went white, brown, white, then brown again, as the sea winds carried in warm or cold air. Some winters even went white, green, white, green. On a peninsula between two large bodies of salt water, "unpredictable" would've been an insult to the weather's inventiveness. As the old folks said, "Yep, ya turns on the radio to find out what the weather was yesterday."

One early afternoon early in the new year, Bonnie was doing her monthly cleaning of Charlie Warner's little house, at the back end of Cannabeck Road. Charlie Warner lived alone, except for his old grey mouser and a couple of dogs who lived mostly outside, and rarely had company. So even though his place only got cleaned once a month, it wasn't all that big a job, except for vacuuming up cat hair. The only complication was that Bonnie had to fit her schedule to Charlie Warner's. He had some sort of millwright or mechanic job in the city, he'd never been very specific about it, and cleaning day could only happen when he had a day off. Most of Bonnie's customers gave her a key to their place, and many even preferred that she do the housecleaning when they weren't there, but not Charlie Warner. He was close to early-retirement age, though, and probably could afford to take it – he certainly didn't seem to've spent-away his wages on extravagances – so maybe all his days would be off soon, and Bonnie wouldn't have to juggle her calendar. Then again, maybe once all his days were off he'd do his own housecleaning. She couldn't imagine how else he'd spend his time, out here on the edge of the woods alone.

As always, Bonnie lugged her gear down into Charlie Warner's basement to begin with – start at the bottom and work your way up. In the basement was a small rec room area, a furnace area Bonnie mostly left alone, and another room Bonnie had never been in. That corner of the basement was walled-off with bargain-grade wood panelling, but tapping on the panelling had told Bonnie it was just the facing for solid concrete, or maybe cinder blocks filled with concrete. The door was painted a cheerful red and was mostly covered by one of those flowery-coloured, cycling-lady posters put out by a nineteenth-century French bicycle company and much reprinted in the 1960s and '70s, and the door handle was the kind of bright brass thumb-latch and hand-clutch types you might see on the door to a solarium. Despite the poster and paint and brass handle, Bonnie suspected it was a steel door. And there was no disguising the very expensive- and serious-looking bolt padlock that needed two keys, on a folded-over hasp that defied prying off, probably all case-hardened steel. Bonnie didn't know exactly what "case-hardened steel" meant, just that it was one of those phrases they used in hardware store catalogues when they really wanted to impress you.

Bonnie thought of that room as "the bunker," although she'd never say that to Charlie Warner. All he'd ever said about it to her, offhandedly on her first day, was, "That's my hobby room, no need for you to go in there."

Bonnie set down her Hoover, and her bucket of cleanser bottles, rags and sponges, on the industrial carpet of Charlie Warner's rec room floor, then went around turning on table lamps and the stand-up, to highlight what the overhead didn't show. One thing the lamps cast new light on was the padlock on the 'hobby room' door. It was hanging loose and open.

Bonnie moved toward the "bunker" door and looked closer at the lock. It was definitely open, hanging from the bolt pulled back out of its housing. She looked to the basement stairs. No one there, and no sound of footsteps. When she'd started down those stairs, Charlie Warner had looked to be well settled-in at his kitchen table, with his pipe and newspaper and a pot of tea. Bonnie looked again at the steel door. She watched her hand come up and take hold of the door handle, then watched her thumb come down on the latch lever. She gave the door a tug.

The instant the door budged a fraction free of its frame, the whole house exploded in sirens and alarm bells. Bonnie wasn't sure if she shrieked, she couldn't hear herself. Charlie Warner came pelting down the stairs, bellowing, "What the hell's going on?" and then, as he charged across the rec room floor, "Get outta the way!" He wasn't a big man, but she had the feeling that if she hadn't dodged out of his way he would've hurled her aside. He threw the door all the way open and jumped inside. Through the doorway, she could see the flashing red lights of a security system panel, then white light as Charlie flicked a switch. He punched a few numbers on the panel's keyboard and the sirens and clanging bells stopped, although Bonnie's ears kept ringing.

Charlie Warner turned away from the panel and said to her through the doorway, "What the *hell* do you think you're doing?"

Bonnie had to gasp a couple of deep breaths before she could say anything. "I'm sorry, Charlie, I, uh, just saw that the lock was off and I –"

"It *was?*"

"Yeah."

Charlie took a step forward to have a look at the lock, then looked down and shook his head. He murmured, "Holy jeez – I must be getting forgetful."

"Well, I didn't know you didn't mean to – I mean, since it wasn't locked this time, I thought maybe you wanted me to go in there and clean that room this time."

"Yeah, I guess you naturally would. I'm sorry, Bonnie, to scare you like that, it's just that . . ." He looked down and shook his head again. "The lock was off. *Damn* – I'm gonna have to make myself a checklist: check myself in and check myself out. Middle-aged fool." Then he looked up and his tone and expression changed. "Well, since you already caught a glimpse I might as well show you." The change reminded Bonnie of something, but she wasn't sure what. Then she placed it: Corporal Kowalchuck, back when she'd told him she knew what had happened with him and Rose. It was the change of someone with a very closely and carefully guarded secret who, when found out, finally has a chance to talk about it.

"A glimpse" was a bit of an exaggeration for as much as Bonnie had seen behind Charlie Warner. But it was enough that she wasn't totally surprised when she stepped into the room. The walls were covered with guns: long guns, handguns, old guns, new guns. The only reason Bonnie knew some of the guns were old was that even someone as uninterested in firearms as she was could tell the difference between a flintlock musket and an assault rifle. Otherwise, the old guns looked just as polished and perfect as the new ones. Bonnie looked from the walls to Charlie Warner. He didn't appear to be anybody's idea of a crazed survivalist, or a dealer in stolen guns: greying blonde hair that was neatly combed but not fussed over, uncomplicated face that was clean-shaven even on a day off. But then, Jack Burton hadn't turned out to bear any resemblance to Henry Silva.

Bonnie went back to looking around the room. In one corner was a workbench with what looked to be the halves of a broken revolver, surrounded by finicky-looking hand tools and calipers. From under the workbench came an annoyed yowl, and out poked the head of the shaggy-shedding grey mouser.

Charlie Warner said to the cat, "It's all right, Nimrod – all secured." Then to Bonnie, "Every couple weeks I shut him in here for a couple hours – make sure no Houdini mice have found a hairline crack in the concrete. Amazing little buggers. That must've been when I forgot to lock the lock back on. Well, you've already met Nimrod, but *this* . . ." He stepped to the workbench, picked up the angled-apart revolver halves, did something with his hands that made a click, and he was holding up a smallish revolver that didn't appear to have ever been broken apart. ". . . is Iver. *One* of the Ivers."

Bonnie said nervously, "Is it loaded?"

"Hell, no. Wouldn't take me but ten seconds, though – I jimmied-up a bracket so you can slot all five shells in at once."

"No, that's all right."

He held the gun up to catch the light. Bonnie could see it was thinner and slightly longer than the one Corporal Kowalchuck took out of Jack Burton's pocket. Charlie said enthusiastically, "You won't see many old Iver Johnson revolvers around, but I've got five of 'em. Manufactured from 1884 to 1917. Feel the weight of it – just like nothing, eh?"

He held it out flat toward her, so Bonnie didn't see much choice but to hold out her hand palm-up. It did feel like a lot less weight than she'd expected.

Charlie Warner gushed on, like an old lady showing off her prize rosebushes. But roses weren't made for killing people. "Small enough to fit in your pocket but solid enough to take the combustion of a .32 cartridge. They called Iver Johnsons 'the workingman's gun,' 'cause they sold pretty cheap but weren't made that way. This model's the Iver Johnson Safety Automatic – but you can see it's a revolver, not an automatic, and it's got no safeties on it. They called it an automatic 'cause, see . . ."

He reached out to take the gun back from her. She didn't mind.

". . . when you break it open and hinge it down to load . . ." He pressed something at the top of the gun, and the barrel and cylinder swung down away from the handle and trigger. ". . . these little push rods come up and automatically eject all the spent cartridges. Pretty nifty, huh?"

"Uh, sure."

"And they called it the Iver Johnson *Safety* Automatic 'cause with the recessed hammer and this little trick with the trigger, you can sit on it or drop it or roll it around in a barrel of marbles – it still won't go off. Elegant piece of engineering." He looked down at it admiringly, then laughed. "One of the Iver Johnson advertising slogans was 'Hammer the Hammer,' 'cause you can beat on the hammer with a hammer, it still won't fire unless you want it to."

Bonnie managed to fake a companionable chuckle, then said, "Uh, do you, uh . . . fire them, or just, you know, look at them?"

"Oh, I've fired 'em all off at least once or twice. You can raise a hood and study on an engine all you like – you still don't really know it till you've driven it around the block a couple of times. There's a little valley a couple miles back in the woods where no one can hear from the road. I even fired off the Kalashnikov there – the AK47." He reached up and lifted down the kind of machine-gun/rifle Bonnie'd seen in many action movies, and in TV news clips from Afghanistan and Iraq and other places. "You know why the AK47 is still the most popular assault rifle in the world, even though the 47 is 'cause it was invented way back in 1947?"

"Uh, no."

"Only six moving parts. Can you beat that? Fully automatic weapon with only *six* moving parts!" Charlie looked down reverently at the assemblage of polished wood and metal in his hands. "Work of goddamned genius." Then his increasingly bright eyes bounced back up to Bonnie. "Say, did you see in the papers a couple years ago poor old Mikhail Kalashnikov himself was in a picture getting a medal from Yeltsin? Or Putin or somebody? Poor old duffer invented the solidest, most-produced assault weapon in the world and never got a patent – that'd be capitalist. But he's still standing there grinning getting his little tin medal for Hero of The Soviet Union."

Bonnie said, "How can you – ? Where do you get all

these?"

Charlie chuckled. "Oh, here and there. For one thing, I do some work down the Boston States from time to time. Last thing customs agents wanna do is dig through a cube van filled with tool boxes and drills and acetylene cylinders and . . . Well, it's gotten dicier the last few years, but there's other ways."

"Say, look at this one!" He put the Kalashnikov on the workbench beside the Iver Johnson, and reached down an odd-looking contraption that looked sort of like a rifle, but with a cylinder like a cowboy's six-gun. "Before Colonel Colt got into handguns he started with revolver-rifles, but there was a little problem with combustion gasses coming back from the cylinder and frying the fingers off whatever poor soldier pulled the trigger . . ."

Bonnie said, "Um, thanks for showing me all this, but I do have to get your house cleaned before I can get home."

"Oh, right." Charlie Warner grinned. "I get a little carried away."

Bonnie went through the afternoon in a daze. As she was lugging her gear back through the kitchen to the back door, Charlie Warner was sitting at his kitchen table again. But now he looked like he'd been sunk into serious second thoughts. He said, "Bonnie, uh, no one else around here knows about . . ." He waved one hand in circles to signify "about you-know-what."

"Yeah, it was just an accident that *I* saw them."

Charlie Warner smiled gratefully and nodded at her with deep relief.

"But, you know," Bonnie added tentatively, "I'm bound to say something about it to Ben, sooner or later."

"Oh, sure. Husbands and wives, just like talking to yourself. Hell, if Big Ben Marsden had a habit of telling tales out of school, half Membertou County'd be in jail."

When Bonnie got home, Ben was in the driveway in his coveralls, walking the snow-scoop back and forth to clear off last night's accumulation. Their first winter in the house, they'd hired a fellow with a four-wheel drive and snowplow, but found out in the spring that their gravel driveway was now pretty much bare earth, and the lawn sprouting gravel. So they'd bought a snow blower that eventually died – Ben had never claimed to be mechanically inclined – and by then Ben had lost his steady job and had more time than money. So it'd been people-power since then, and Ben claimed it helped keep him in shape through January, when odd jobs were thin on the ground.

When Bonnie climbed out of the car, Ben started chuckling, as though he'd been waiting to tell her something funny. With half an eye still on the snow-scoop he was pushing, he said loud enough to be heard over the scrape and swoosh, "Fergus was by for a bit. Called and said 'Whatcha up to?' I said, 'Just washing the dishes. What are you doin'?' He said, 'I just finished doin' the laundry, figured I'd drop by for a beer.' I said, 'Okay.' It wasn't till after I hung up I realized . . ." Now Ben laughed outright. "Here's these two roughneck, redneck country boys, 'Whatcha doin'? Washing dishes, doing the laundry, figured I'd drop by for a beer.'"

Ben raised his eyes off the snow-scoop to look directly at Bonnie, and his laugh faded. He said, "What happened? You look like you seen a ghost."

"I have. Or the makings of some."

"Huh?"

"It's a bit of a long story for standing around in the cold."

"Well, I was thinking it was about time I took a break anyway."

By the time Ben had got out of his coveralls and boots, and clumped back upstairs from feeding the furnace, Bonnie had a pot of tea steeping on the kitchen table. As Ben sat down across from her, Bonnie said, "The house I was cleaning this afternoon was Charlie Warner's, back on Cannabeck Road. You know him?"

"Not much. He's got some sort of machinist job in the city."

"That's right."

Ben shrugged. "Bumped into him once or twice. Kind of ee-centric, but that's no crime."

"You don't know the half of it . . ."

When Bonnie'd finished telling Ben what had happened, he

didn't exactly react in a way she'd expected. He just chuckled and said, "I wondered what Charlie Warner did with his spare time. Nobody hardly ever sees him except when he's driving into the city to work or driving home. But I figured he must have at least a couple old antique guns, 'cause a couple of the guys were saying –"

"He's got an *arsenal* in there!"

"Oh for God's sakes, Bonnie – he's a millwright, they're just machines to him. Verna Parker collects quilts; that doesn't mean she plans to smother little children with them."

"There's no legal requirements to be a quilt collector. I'm damned sure Charlie Warner isn't a registered gun collector."

"And damned smart he is not to be." Ben got up to pour a little something in his tea. "Otherwise he'd be up to his neck in bullshit with the Federal Gun Registry."

Bonnie let that one lie. A few years ago she'd convinced him to register his few hunting guns by the deadline when the Federal Gun Registry came into being. Then once he'd registered and paid his fees, the deadline got moved back again and again, and the fees got dropped again and again – no refunds for fees already paid – and the whole national program turned into a national mess costing hundreds of millions more tax dollars than it was supposed to. Bonnie knew Ben still took a fair bit of ribbing at the firehall for having been such a good boy. And now the government was going to do away with the long gun registry altogether, so anyone who'd filled out all those forms and paid out all that money was even more of a good fool.

Ben said, "You know, it could well be that there's some mechanical doohickey that makes your life easier, that came about because Charlie Warner was looking at the mechanism of one of his guns and said to hisself, 'Hey, that little spring and sprocket idea'd work just dandy for the shifter on a lawnmower,' or whatever."

"Those guns might be just interesting machinery to Charlie Warner, but not necessarily to anybody else who got their hands on them."

"How's anybody else gonna get their hands on them? Millwright like him – you said yourself that padlock isn't the kind you can pry off with a crowbar. And I betcha ten dollars there's bars on any windows in that room."

"There aren't any windows."

"There, you see? And he's got a couple of big dogs, doesn't he?"

"Well, yeah . . ." Bonnie got the feeling Ben was leading her somewhere she didn't want to be led, but facts were facts. "That's one of the reasons I have to time cleaning his house for days when he isn't away working. He's got the yard and some of the woods out back page-wired, so when he leaves he just lets the dogs run loose. A pair of mastiffs."

"*Mastiffs?*" Ben laughed. "Couple years ago I was helping old Cyril whipper-snip his front ditch, when a pickup truck went by with a mastiff in the back. I asked old Cyril – he knows most there is to know about dogs – 'I know what they bred Lab retrievers for, and beagles, and Irish wolfhounds, but what are mastiffs bred for?' And he said," Ben imitated old Cyril's crackly, matter-of-fact voice, "'Killing people.'"

Bonnie didn't laugh, although Ben left room as though he expected her to.

"So, uh," Ben went on, after his 'funny' story fell flat, "what with the dogs and the lock and the steel door and all – I don't think you have to worry about somebody getting their hands on Charlie Warner's gun collection."

"He forgot to lock the door."

"Well, he didn't forget to turn the alarm on, did he?" Ben picked up his tea mug and tilted it all the way back to get the dregs. "Damn, I wish I could tell the guys at the firehall about Charlie Warner's hobby – be a great story. But, with that good a story, once a few people know, everybody knows." He got up and put his tea mug in the sink. "I can prob'ly finish up the driveway before suppertime. If we don't get a melt soon, I'm gonna run out of places to pile the snow."

Ben seemed to believe that the subject was dealt with and

closed; Bonnie wasn't so sure. After he'd gone back outside, she poured herself another cup of tea and sat smoking a cigarette. She kept hearing what Corporal Kowalchuck had said about Jack Burton's gun: *"pocket revolver . . . almost an antique . . ."*

Enough happened in the next few days to push the subject to the back of her mind. Over and above the regular round of things that more than occupied Bonnie's time, Ben got his "melt" – more than he bargained for. Three feet of snow melting in two days, sitting on top of ground that was still frozen, made for a lot of water with no place to go but to flow in the path of least resistance. The run-off on both sides of the house just flowed down to the stream, but there was a lot of uphill straight in front of the house. So Bonnie and Ben put in a number of hours frantically chipping the ice out of the baby drainage ditch that horseshoed the front of the house. One advantage to living on a hill was that water that seeped in through the front of the basement just flowed out the back basement door. Which would've been fine if the basement had been just a basement, but the only way they'd been able to make that old bungalow big enough for a family was to build rooms in the basement, with sub-floors and carpets and gyprock walls and insulation.

When they'd finally got the moat cleared, and stood watching the water flowing beautifully out the ends, Ben looked around at the new green grass taking over from the white, and said, "This won't last. Winter'll be back."

Bonnie said, "Yeah, but maybe this time it won't leave as rudely," and Ben laughed.

The next morning, Bonnie and Ben were making breakfast and half-listening to an endangered species: one of the last small, locally owned radio stations in existence. Bonnie half heard *"Turning to the local news . . ."* and then started paying more attention.

"There was a tragic accident in Membertou County last evening. Two fourteen-year-old boys were back in the woods shooting tin cans with an old revolver. Through a mishandling accident, one of the boys was shot."

Bonnie murmured, "What a sin."

"Fourteen-year-old Harvey Bullard of Bullard's Road remains in Intensive Care. According to RCMP, the boys said they found the old revolver in the woods. The investigation continues. On a lighter note, the Membertou County High School Swim Team is holding a fund-raising –"

Bonnie switched off the radio, put down her egg-whipper and went to the kitchen doorway to call, "Melissa!"

Melissa's voice came from the bathroom down the hall. "I'm getting ready!"

"Just come into the kitchen for a minute, honey – then you can keep on getting ready."

"In a minute!"

Bonnie went back to mixing chopped green onions and peppers into the eggs she was scrambling. She said to Ben, "Funny your pager didn't go off, if there was an emergency just up on Bullard's Road." Ben had taken the First Responder's course at the Volunteer Fire Department, and was known to grumble about letting the chief talk him into it.

"Probably the emergency never got called in. Probably the kid's folks just threw him in the car and lit out for the hospital." Ben went back to carefully carving thin slices off the half-side of bacon they'd got smoke-cured by a widow whose eyesight wasn't good enough to give her home a proper cleaning, but still good enough to operate her smokehouse. Bonnie suspected that the old girl's failing vision had something to do with tending the smokehouse all those years. Ben muttered as he sliced, "Poor kid."

Melissa appeared in the kitchen doorway, with one half of her amber hair combed out and the other not quite. "Why do I have to come into the kitchen?"

Bonnie turned away from the egg bowl again – it was all pretty much mixed anyway. "Just for a minute, honey. Do you know a boy named Harvey Bullard?"

"No – he's in Big School, 'cross the road. But his sister's in my class. Why?"

"Well, I didn't want you to hear it first on the school bus. Harvey Bullard's had a bad accident; he's in the hospital."

"What kind of ack-sidden?"

"Well, it seems Harvey Bullard and a friend of his found an old gun in the woods and were playing with it –"

"That was stupid."

"Melissa! If somebody's had a bad accident, you don't say 'that was stupid.' You wait for them to say it."

"Why? If it *was* stupid . . ."

Bonnie could hear Ben's eyebrows raising across the room. She crouched down in front of her youngest, put her hands on the tiny shoulders, and tried to think of a way to explain a pronouncement on proper behaviour she'd gone and made before she'd even had her second cup of coffee. "Um . . . You remember back a couple of years ago when we told you the ice was too thin to play on the pond, but you went down there anyway and fell through?"

"It wasn't deep enough to drown."

"Yeah, but it sure was cold, wasn't it? How would you have liked it if when I came running down to pull you out I'd said, 'That was stupid'? You already knew that." Melissa looked like maybe what her mother was saying might make some sort of sense. "Now you'd better hurry and finish getting ready or you won't have time for breakfast before the school bus."

Ben had already started the bacon cooking. Bonnie waited for him to finish, so she could pour most of the grease out of the skillet and do the eggs. She said, "Bullard's Road runs parallel to Cannabeck Road, doesn't it?"

"More or less – other side of the hill." He spoke abstractedly, concentrating on turning sizzling strips so they'd come out crisp but not charcoaled. "Couple miles of woods between them."

"The same woods where Charlie Warner takes his 'machinery' to drive it around the block."

"He wouldn't just leave them lying around in the woods. They're his babies, from what you said."

"He wouldn't *mean* to leave them lying around in the woods. He didn't mean to leave that door unlocked."

"Bonnie, that revolver coulda come from anywhere. There's

more old guns lying around attics in Membertou County than you want to think about."

"And how many are lying around the woods between Charlie Warner's place and Bullard's Road? And Harvey Bullard's little sister is in Melissa's class." She hoped that would get across to Ben that this was getting pretty close to home.

All it seemed to get across to him was to remind him that Melissa was within overhearing distance. He lowered his voice to the volume they'd long ago learned wouldn't carry out of a room. "All that you *know* about Charlie Warner is that he's a harmless, careful kind of guy who spends his lonesome hours studying up on a kind of machinery the government don't want him to have." He turned his attention to the bacon again, then back to her. "You can't go around getting . . . welcomed into people's houses to do a job of work for them, and then snooping through their closets to find some reason to turn them in to the police."

"I've done that before, and you said you were glad I did."

"Sure – when you know for *sure* somebody's doing something that's hurting somebody else. All you know for sure about *this* is that Charlie Warner collects old guns, and some kid who lives two or three miles from him had an accident with an old gun. Bacon's ready."

Partway through breakfast, Ben said, "Well, I'm guessing the firehall parking lot's an unholy mess and'll need some drainage dug – be a skating rink if they don't get the melt-off run off before it freezes again. Won't bring us in any money, but they'll feed me a free lunch, and there ain't much use having emergency vehicles in the village if they can't get out to the road. And what've *you* got on today, Bonnie's Cleaning Service?"

"Just the Senator's house. Sometimes it takes me all day, so I don't book anybody else."

The look Ben trained on her, and his tone of voice, weren't nearly as breezy as the surface of the conversation might seem. "So that's *all* you're going to do today."

"Yeah. That's all I'm going to do."

The Senator was officially retired, to a big, lovely house and grounds on the Fundy shore. But, given some of the visitors who passed through, and the number of trips the Senator still took to Ottawa, Bonnie wondered if people that involved in politics ever really retired. Today, though, although the Senator and his wife weren't off on a trip, they weren't home, either. So Bonnie turned the stereo system on to the local radio station through all the speakers throughout the house, after first penciling a note of what station the radio had been tuned to and which speakers had been set. She turned it up loud enough that she could even hear it over the vacuum cleaner, more or less, at least the music parts. She had just finished vacuuming the sunroom as a cheerful old Hank Snow song ended, and was moving on to the half-wall of windows facing the bay, when the announcer came on, not sounding cheerful at all.

"I'm afraid I have some sad news to report. Harvey Bullard, the young man we reported earlier was in Intensive Care after being badly wounded in a shooting accident, has passed away. Counselling will be available for students at Membertou County High School and Piziquid Village Elementary."

Bonnie wandered in a daze into the living room where the stereo controls were, turned off the radio and slumped into the nearest chair. She sat there limply for a while, feeling like a bit of flotsam caught in a cross-current. Her eyes eventually focused on an antique telephone table across the room, with a definitely not antique phone on it. She got up and crossed the room, pulled out the telephone table's low-backed chair and sat down again. She said to herself, *If there's no phone book, I won't.*

She pulled open the telephone table's drawer, and there was the local phone book. She looked up and keyed-in the number, saying to herself, *If he's not there, I'll leave it alone.* He was there. As she waited for the receptionist to transfer her call to his office, Bonnie said to herself, *If it was just any old gun, I won't.*

"Corporal Kowalchuck, Membertou County RCMP."

"Corporal, it's Bonnie Marsden . . ."

"Oh hello, Bonnie. What can I do for you today?"

"Um . . ." *How to begin, without getting in too deep to pull out?* "Well, I just heard on the radio that Harvey Bullard died, the boy shot in the accident . . . ?"

There was a small pause. Bonnie could hear Corporal Kowalchuck wondering why she would call him to tell him something he already knew. Then he just said, "Yes."

"And I was wondering . . . They said on the radio the boys were shooting tin cans with an old revolver. Do you happen to know what kind of revolver it was? I mean, was it just any old revolver, or an antique?"

"What difference does it make?"

"Well . . . Let's just say it's something I'd like to know. Maybe I heard something, or maybe I'm just imagining things."

"Hm." Another small pause for him to weigh considerations, then, "There's a lot of things you've wanted to know around Membertou County, Bonnie, and a lot of them have turned out to be very helpful to me. So . . . It's no big secret, just a detail that wouldn't get into the newspapers, or onto the radio. The firearm in question was a .32 calibre handgun manufactured around 1900 by the Iver Johnson company."

"I thought they were supposed to be safe, and can't go off by accident."

"And how would you happen to know that?"

"Oh, it's just . . . something I heard somebody say once."

That sounded pretty lame, even to her. This time the pause was longer. She could tell his suspicion radar was blipping: so far she'd told him nothing and he'd told her something. But, it seemed he decided to let it go. "My information is that this particular model *was* known as a Safety Automatic, even though it's a revolver. But there's no such thing as a safe loaded gun, Bonnie. Even trigger locks aren't entirely reliable."

"You're certain that the gun was an Iver Johnson?"

"No question. I tagged it myself for the inquest."

Bonnie took in and held a deep breath, as though she was about to dive into deep water, and she was. "Corporal, I've got something to tell you . . ."

8

Corporal Kowalchuck stood beside his vehicle parked at the sharp bend just before the end of Cannabeck Road, listening to the sounds of the false spring in Membertou County: crows and squirrels, whispering pines, the barking of two large dogs around the bend. And the barking of the sergeant in command of the Emergency Response Team into his radio mike: "Ten-four. Ten-twelve." Which meant the sergeant had just told his team *Affirmative* and *Stand by*. The sergeant told Corporal Kowalchuck, "The sharpshooters are in position."

Corporal Kowalchuck refrained from saying, *Oh, goody*. On the one hand, he knew he was lucky that the ERT hadn't had much to do lately, which meant that they'd been available to back him up on very short notice. On the other hand, the inactivity meant they were a bit excited about finally having something to do. 'Excited' wasn't an adjective Kowalchuck liked applied to police officers, or the people they had to deal with. What Kowalchuck did say was, "You're sure they weren't seen?"

"My men are very good at their jobs, Corporal. And with this bend in the road, and the ridge, we could be mounting the D-Day invasion without the suspect knowing."

Kowalchuck refrained from saying, *We're not?* Instead, he said, "Did your constable say whether the pair of mastiffs are shut in their pen or running loose?"

"In their pen."

"Good." Although it wasn't all that good. It meant an option Kowalchuck had been half-considering was still open to him. "It's very reassuring to have your team along, Sergeant, but you're probably wasting your time. My information is that the suspect is just a collector, not some kind of paranoid survivalist."

"Your information may be incorrect."

"I guess there's one way to find out."

"What's that?"

Kowalchuck started divesting himself of his coat, kevlar vest and uniform cap and piling them on the car hood. "I'll go knock on his door."

The sergeant said, "What the hell do you think you're doing?"

"Wouldn't *you* get kind of nervous seeing an armed man in body armour walking up your driveway?" Kowalchuck added his ordnance belt to the pile. "And given the amount of weaponry Mr. Warner supposedly has in there, my sidearm isn't going to accomplish anything but make him uncomfortable."

"I *am* the ranking officer here, Corporal."

"I'm well aware of that, Sergeant – but your team was only called in as back-up and this *is* my jurisdiction." Actually, it was a dicey question whether rank or jurisdiction took precedence. So Kowalchuck added, "Do you *want* this to turn into a firefight?"

"Of course not."

"Well, an unarmed officer knocking on his front door is less likely to get Mr. Warner's dander up, than somebody blaring at him through a megaphone to come out with his hands in the air."

The sergeant chewed on that for a short moment, then nodded, "Ten-four, Corporal."

"Ten-twelve." Kowalchuck turned to start walking down the road. "I'll wave you in when the situation is secured."

"I hope so."

Not near as much as I do, passed through Kowalchuck's mind. The gravel crunching under his boots seemed a very lonely sound once he'd got around the bend. It wasn't exactly shirtsleeves weather, but not too brisk as long as he walked briskly. He seemed to remember being in this kind of situation before: walking forward unarmed and unarmoured, to put himself in front of someone who was armed and possibly dangerous. Then he placed it. Rose Coffin holding a rifle on the person who'd murdered someone who'd once saved Rose's life at great cost to his own, and in those circumstances Rose hadn't been *possibly* dangerous. Well, that situation had resolved itself all right. Barely.

As he got nearer to the little green house at the end of the road, Kowalchuck could see the high page wire surrounding the yard, and that there was a long gate between one front corner of the house and the fence – the kind of gate farmers and horse people put across their entrance roads. Behind that gate were the two mastiffs, looking and sounding like they were going to chew through the gate to get at the intruder. Kowalchuck was surprised that Charles Warner hadn't stepped outside to see what was driving his dogs crazy. But then again, living on the edge of the woods, his dogs probably often went crazy about a passing racoon or skunk or deer.

As Kowalchuck opened the smaller gate to the flagstoned front path, he noticed an electrical contact beside the latch and an insulated wire running down the gatepost to disappear under the ground. Whatever kind of buzzer or bell the wire was rigged to, anyone inside the house definitely knew now that what was driving the dogs crazy wasn't a passing forest creature.

When Kowalchuck got within a few steps of the front step, working his cheekbone muscles to squeeze some saliva into his parchment-dry mouth, the front door opened. Out stepped a not very large man of late middle age and neat appearance. He didn't look particularly threatening, but he was wearing a baggy, thick sweater-coat that might be concealing all manner of articles. The gentleman said, "Hello. I saw you coming up the drive." Kowalchuck knew that wasn't how the gentleman had been alerted to his presence, but it didn't matter. "Somebody lost in the woods?"

"Are you Charles Warner?"

The man on the doorstep angled his head and looked confused. It looked to Kowalchuck that the confusion wasn't over the question itself, but why a police officer would ask him that. The gentleman said warily, "Yeah."

Mr. Warner didn't ask the nice policeman to step inside and explain, and Kowalchuck had no doubt it wasn't accidental that Mr. Warner had chosen to intercept him at the front step, instead of waiting for him to come to the door. Charles Warner obviously knew enough about the law to know that police officers are like vampires: they can't cross your threshold unless invited, but once invited, your premises are theirs. Not unless invited, unless: "I have a warrant to search your house."

"*What?*" Charles Warner flapped his arms. "What for?"

"*Please* leave your arms down by your sides, Mr. Warner. And don't reach into your pockets."

Mr. Warner dropped his arms and squinted at the woods and the ridge across the road. He said in almost a whisper, "Sharpshooters?"

"Uh-huh." Kowalchuck realized the positive side of Mr. Warner choosing to intercept him at the front step. Now that Charles Warner was out in the open, Kowalchuck had more reason to worry about Mr. Warner's safety than his own. Not that that didn't have its negative side. "I think you know what we're searching for, Mr. Warner – illegal firearms."

"But . . ." Charles Warner's face screwed up like a winter apple doll. ". . . this is my *home*. You can't just – I never hurt anybody! I pay my taxes! I never even drive through orange lights! You can't just walk in here and –"

"*Please*, Mr. Warner – try not to move your hands around."

Charles Warner's expression and manner changed again, as though he'd found a straw to clutch. "A warrant won't stand up just on suspicion. If you don't have some sort of hard information, any search'll get thrown out in court."

"I am very well aware of that."

Mr. Warner looked sceptical of Kowalchuck's certainty, then seemed to be considering the possibilities of where the police might've got some hard information, then shook his head. "Nah. Nobody knows – at least nobody who ain't in on the same hobby." Then his head jolted back, as if "hobby" had flipped a switch. His head lolled forward and his whole body went slack. He muttered, "Why'd she have to go and . . . ." He raised his head a little and said dully, "What am I looking at, Corporal – ten years?"

"If you continue to cooperate, the judge might well –"

"Are you kidding me? The way people are screaming about guns these days? Any judge that doesn't throw the book at me'll have the newspapers all over him! And I sure as hell ain't gonna 'cooperate' as far as ratting out on anybody." That seemed to've been about as much spirit as he had left in him. "Oh, hell. Is it all right if I get something out of my pocket?"

"Very slowly."

"Might help if you held your hand out like you're expecting me to put something in it – which I'm gonna."

Kowlachuck held out his right hand, palm up. Charles Warner slowly delved into his trousers pocket, came out with something that jingled, and put it in Kowalchuck's hand. It was two keys, not the kind that could be copied at the neighbourhood hardware store, on a small, looseleaf ring.

Charles Warner said, "Keys to the padlock – save you the trouble of trying to break down a steel door and probably crushing my cat."

"Thank you."

Mr. Warner said in a lost voice, as though something had just occurred to him, "Who's gonna take care of my boys?"

Kowalchuck was about to say something intelligent like *Huh?* since he was under the impression that Mr. Warner lived alone, with no dependent children. Then he realized Charles Warner meant the cat and the dogs. Kowalchuck said, "I'm sure that some, uh, arrangements can be made," then raised his right arm in the air and waved his hand forward, to bring in the sergeant and *his* boys.

* * *

Ben was leaned back in the firehall lounge sipping a beer and feeling the feeling come back into his wool-socked toes, after several hours of mud-soaked boots and drainage ditches. There seemed to be some sort of commotion developing around the radio room. Young Reid Olson was leaned in the radio room doorway, and said something over his shoulder to the two guys at the pool table that made them put down their cues and go over to him. Ben got up and padded across the carpet to the radio room doorway. He could see over shoulders that big Darlene Porter, the only female full member of the Piziquid Village VFD, was at the console, and had the book of civic addresses open in front of her. He could hear that she was tuned to the Mountie radio. He said to the guys at the doorway, "What's up?"

Reid said, "Oh, hey, Ben. The Mounties've been doing some big operation, SWAT team and sniffer dogs and all. They kept off the dispatch frequency till they got the job done, but now they're talking."

Darlene Porter closed the book of civic addresses and said over her shoulder, "It's the last house on Cannabeck Road. Charles Warner."

Reid said, "Old Charlie Warner? What the hell would he be . . . ?"

Someone else said, "Charlie ain't *that* old, young fella."

Ben didn't say anything.

Darlene Porter said, "Now they're calling for a cube van, to load up evidence."

Someone said, "That's a hell of a lot of evidence."

Reid said, "Maybe a growhouse?"

Someone else said, "Nah, not Charlie Warner."

"Maybe a still?"

Ben backed away from the group, set his beer down on the nearest horizontal surface, and went to the side door where his boots were sitting on a rack. He was moving neither fast nor slow, and seemed to be piloting himself from outside. His whole body was numb and tingling at the same time. He drove home carefully, aware that his right foot wanted to jam down on the gas pedal, and his hands wanted to yank the steering wheel from side to side. Bonnie's car was in the driveway. Clyde barked hello as Ben walked from the truck to the house. Ben waved back half-heartedly and muttered, "Yeah, Clyde, nice day."

As Ben kicked off his boots in the mudroom, he called, "Bonnie!"

"I'm in the kitchen! Tea's on."

Ben stumped up the stairs, saying, "Leave it on." He stopped at the top of the stairs and looked at his wife. She was sitting primly at the kitchen table, looking like Little Miss Muffet the Spider Squasher. He said, "Firehall radio picked up a lot of activity on the Mountie radio. SWAT team, sniffer dogs, cube van to haul away evidence . . . All down at Charlie Warner's place. You wouldn't happen to know anything about that, would you?"

She didn't seem all that perturbed by the question, more like he just didn't know the whole story. "Ben, I checked to be sure before I said anything. The gun that killed that boy was an Iver Johnson – the same rare kind Charlie Warner was showing off to me."

"Charlie Warner could get five to ten years in penitentiary, because you made a little phone call."

"It wouldn't be that much."

"That much or more! Automatic weapons smuggled across the border?" She seemed to be impossibly far away, even just across the kitchen. He wondered if maybe it'd always been that way, and maybe all those years they'd got along together because they'd been so occupied with raising three kids and shoring up the house and Bonnie working overtime at the credit union. Ben tried to think of some way to get across to her. "When I had to spend six *weeks* in jail it just about drove me crazy. Five to ten *years*? By the time Charlie Warner gets out, there won't be anything left of him."

"There *isn't* anything left of Harvey Bullard, except a funeral. Next time it could've been Melissa out playing in the woods and stumbling across – There she is."

"Huh?" Ben looked at the clock; not school bus time yet. But when he looked to the front door, he could see down the slant of the stairs the top of Melissa's red toque as she closed the door behind her.

Bonnie got up and moved to the kitchen doorway, calling, "Hello, honey, how did you get home?"

Melissa called back, apparently busy taking off her boots and coat, "Cindy's mom came to get her early and I asked could I get a ride home and teacher said okay."

As Melissa came up the stairs, Bonnie said, "Would you like some apple juice and cheese?"

"No, thanks." It came out kind of limp and listless, like Melissa wasn't really there, and that was the way she was moving, too.

Bonnie said, "How about some milky tea with honey?"

"Okay."

As Bonnie busied herself with tea, milk and honey, and Melissa flopped onto a chair, Ben said, trying to sound cheerful, "Hello, pumpkin."

"Hello, Daddy."

Bonnie said from her mixing station at the counter, not casually, "How did things go at school?"

"A lotta kids were crying. We had a sembly. They asked me if I wanted to talk to a Toronto counsellor, but –"

"A Toronto counsellor?" Bonnie turned from the counter perplexedly, then, "Oh, a *trauma* counsellor."

"You told me the right way to say it was Toe-ron-toe."

At another time, Ben would've found that funny, wee Melissa out-logicking her mother. But nothing seemed particularly funny just now.

Bonnie said, "That's a different word, honey – that's for Geography. But that doesn't matter just now. They asked you if you wanted to talk to a trauma counsellor?"

"And I said if I wanted to talk to somebody I'd talk to my friends." Bonnie set the cup down in front of Melissa, and Melissa didn't say thank you. Ben didn't figure today was a day for Miss Manners, and apparently Bonnie didn't, either. "Mommy, what do you do if somebody whispers you something you should maybe tell the teacher, or the police, but it's a secret?"

Bonnie looked more than a bit taken aback. She sat down kitty corner to her daughter and said, "Um, I'm not sure what you mean, honey."

"Well, at lunchtime, Harvey Bullard's sister was sitting way off in the corner of the playground 'cause nobody knew what to say to her. So I went up and we were talking and she whispered . . . It was a lie that Harvey Bullard and his friend found the gun in the woods. Harvey Bullard's grandfather gave it to him to go shooting."

Bonnie's head jerked back like Melissa had thrown the milky tea in her face. She sputtered, "*What?* Why would . . .? How could anybody be so crazy as giving a fourteen-year-old boy a loaded pistol to play with?"

Ben said flatly, not trusting himself to let any kind of emotion or expressiveness into his voice, "That's probably how old the grandfather was when *his* old man gave it to him for target-shooting. He just didn't think of the fact that fourteen-year-old boys now aren't as grown up as they had to be back then." He turned to Melissa. "I know you asked your mother, pumpkin, but I'll put in my two cents' worth.

"Seems to me that Harvey Bullard's grandfather is probably punishing himself more than the law ever could, but that's just what I think." He moved toward the kitchen doorway. "Now I'll go pour myself a drink, and you two sort out what *you* think."

Bonnie's voice came from behind him, "Ben?"

Ben kept on heading for the basement stairs, tossing over his shoulder, "Your daughter's got a problem she wants you to sort out."

* * *

It took Bonnie some untangling to sort out an answer to Melissa's question. She finally managed to convince Melissa, and herself, that in this particular, singular situation it was up to the Bullard family to decide whether to say where Harvey had actually got the gun. And that Melissa wouldn't be lying to anybody by not telling the Bullards' secret; she just wouldn't be telling. Then she managed to convince Melissa that Clyde really, really wanted someone to throw a stick for him. Provided that someone didn't throw it past the reach of his line so he'd strangle himself running after it.

As soon as Melissa was out the door, Bonnie heaved herself out of her chair and down the basement stairs. Her body felt a good deal heavier than it had that morning. Ben wasn't in the rec room. He was in the bedroom, taking clothes and things out of his dresser drawers and stuffing them into his old blue duffle bag laid out on the bed. He'd always been very pleased with that duffle bag. Unlike most duffle bags, it had a zipper all down the side, so you could get at things without rummaging from the top or emptying the whole bag out. And, like most duffle bags, you could pack in things like bottles or flashlights and pad around them with clothes and towels. At the moment, what he was stuffing into the bag was the fuzzy burgundy sweater she'd given him a few Christmases ago and he'd said was too flashy and then wore it all the time.

Bonnie said, "What are you doing?"

He said drily, without looking at her, "What's it look like? I got enough clothes throwed together for a few days, and I'll put enough tools on the truck for the job I'm starting on tomorrow."

She still wasn't exactly sure what he was saying. She said, "Where are you going?"

Still carrying on with his packing, and still not looking at her, Ben said, "I don't know. Not far. I'll take my keys so's I can get into the house and the barn and get whatever else I need when I can see your car's not here. There's enough in the bank to pay next month's mortgage, and I'll leave you money in an envelope when I get some."

Now that he'd made himself abundantly clear, the unfairness of it was infuriating. "I don't make the laws, Ben!"

"Yeah, well, that's what those two sleazy undercover agents

said when I got nailed six weeks in jail for having a pint of moonshine in my barn."

Bonnie could feel the heat rising in her face. "That's a hell of a thing to say to me."

"That's a hell of a thing you just *did*. You just flushed Charlie Warner's life down the toilet."

"You don't *know* that. They might only confiscate his guns and give him a few months in jail."

"*Only?*" Ben stopped and looked at her now, but it wasn't a pleasant kind of look. "Why should they do *anything* to him? What'd he ever do to you, or to anybody else?"

"But next time it might've been one of *his* guns that –"

"Don't give me *might've been!*" Ben's huge hands fisted and vibrated. Then he lowered his hands, and his voice. "The last thing you said to me this morning was you weren't going to do anything today but clean the Senator's house."

"I meant work."

"You know damn well it meant more'n that."

"That was before Harvey Bullard died, and I found out the gun was an Iver Johnson."

"You couldn't have waited a couple of hours to talk to me about it?"

"What – I need your *permission?*"

"No, but you used to need my *opinion*. Seems like you don't need anybody's opinion anymore, except your own, and what the official law tells you is right and wrong."

"That isn't true."

"I don't know anymore." Ben looked down at his lump-stuffed duffle bag and started to zip it up. "You did what you did."

"And this is how you're punishing me for it?"

"I ain't punishing anybody. Just, right now, lying down in the same bed with you tonight wouldn't feel very comfortable. I gotta go away and think about that for a while." He hefted the duffle bag and started for the doorway.

"But . . ." Bonnie couldn't think of anything to say but,

"What'll I tell Melissa?"

Ben brushed past her and out, saying without looking back, "Oh, you'll figure out something. You're good at telling people things."

9

Ben didn't come back home that night, or the next day, or the next. Bonnie was back to sleeping with a lengthwise pillow beside her, as she had for those long forty nights when Ben was in jail. The feel of something against her back, or her side, or under her arm – depending on which way she rolled over in her sleep – made it slightly less likely that she'd wake up in a panic in the middle of the night. And these nights were a lot worse than the ones in the fall. At least with those forty nights she'd been able to count them off on the calendar, and there'd been some outside reason for it all, instead of something inside her and her husband.

Bonnie booked as much work as she could scare up, sometimes undercutting herself, to get out of the house and keep herself occupied. She switched some bookings around to days when the homeowners couldn't be there, in case she got ambushed by another uncontrollable urge to just sit down and cry.

Some days when Bonnie got home from work, Ben had been there to do his laundry or pick up some extra clothes or tools, and he'd've moved some firewood into the basement, or maybe shovelled the driveway wider than what she'd managed to clear from the latest snowfall. As often as not, he'd've left an envelope with some money towards next month's mortgage, and one Wednesday a note he'd pick up Melissa when school got out on Friday and take her to McDonald's. The only other note he'd left, the first time Bonnie'd come home to find he'd been there, was that anyone who wanted to get ahold of him could leave a message at MacGuigans' gas station. Bonnie'd heard from here and there that Ben was living at the MacGuigans' hunting camp, a few miles outside the village, and she suspected he was picking up the odd shift covering for one of the MacGuigans at the service station. Ben had always said he was better with wood than machinery, but he could pump gas and change an oil filter.

Bonnie decided she wasn't going to try and get ahold of him unless there was some immediate, practical reason. He was the one who'd walked out.

The reason the Mounties had had to search Charlie Warner's house was judged legitimate 'In Chambers,' whatever that meant. What it meant to Bonnie was that her name didn't come out in public. Not that she thought she'd done anything wrong, but Charlie Warner's arrest and trial had become a subject of hot disagreements in kitchens and coffee shops, and the sides weren't neatly divided between men and women. As it was, the neighbours didn't know Bonnie'd had anything to do with it, nor why exactly Ben had moved away from her. Or did they? Sometimes Bonnie caught someone looking at her sideways down a grocery aisle.

Jack Burton's trial was another matter. Bonnie had no doubt Ben had been subpoenaed to testify, since she had, and even Darcy. The trial was set for the Nova Scotia Supreme Court, in downtown Halifax. Since Piziquid Village was more than fifty kilometres from there – barely – Bonnie was entitled to basic travel expenses, so she assumed Ben was, too. *Very* basic, but with the price of gas these days, and of even a sandwich lunch in the city, doing their civic duty would've been expensive without a little cushion. Bonnie thought for a minute about getting a message to Ben that they should travel together, instead of burning gas in two vehicles. But only for a minute.

Bonnie and Darcy were subpoenaed for the third day of the trial; the first two days were taken up with the Crown's and

Defence's opening arguments, and the tabling of some technical evidence. The Crown attorney had told Bonnie, in their pre-interview, that there were some odd little details about the burned-out wreck of Billy Vickers's car that didn't seem to fit with an engine fire or gas leak. The details hadn't been enough on their own to build a case, but gave some back-up for the case Bonnie had tricked Jack Burton into building against himself. One of the odd details was that although the transmission was in neutral and the park brake on, the driver's seat belt buckle was still fastened. That gave Bonnie a bit of a shiver, since she'd imagined out of thin air Jack Burton saying, *Glad to see you were wearing your seat belt. Safety first.*

Bonnie picked up Darcy on her way in through the city to the courthouse. There was a metal detector at the courthouse door, and beyond it a wide, long hallway or lobby that echoed with the hiss and murmur of small groups of people whispering and muttering. It seemed to Bonnie that some of the muted voices were coming out of the slate stones of the floor and dingy plaster of the walls.

The blue-uniformed gatekeeper at the courtroom entrance was a big black woman with a big smile that looked like it could turn upside-down in an instant. She checked their names on her clipboard, then said, "Well, there's no exclusion order, as there usually is, especially first-degree murder. Usually the Crown or Defence or both want the witnesses excluded till they're called for testimony, so they can't hear what the witnesses before them said. I guess since today's witnesses are all the same family, they figured you'd know what each other is gonna say anyway."

Bonnie chose not to say anything to that.

"So, you can go inside, or wait in the lobby till you're called, up to you. But, if you go inside, you'll have to stay there till a recess is called."

Bonnie looked at Darcy, who shrugged, "Not much going on out here."

The first thing Bonnie saw when they stepped into the courtroom was the back of a very large head with grey-flecked, red-brown hair. It was in the last row back from the fence out front, and of course the aisle seat, so Ben had room to put his legs. Apparently he'd been listening for people coming in and down the aisle, because he pulled his feet out of the way and looked up. His eyes hit Bonnie's and bounced off. He nodded hello, but Bonnie wasn't sure if he was nodding at her and Darcy, or just Darcy. Bonnie nodded back politely anyway, and kept on going.

They found two seats near the front and waited. On the other side of the fence in front of the civilians were two tables facing the judge's dais. At one table was the bald spot at the back of the Crown Prosecutor's head, hunched over some papers. His thin shoulders were draped in a black court robe instead of the grey, off-the-rack suit she'd seen him in before, the kind favoured by men more interested in durability than pizzaz. Bonnie had learned a lot about reading clothing in her years as a loans officer, and the Crown prosecutor's office-wear was definitely a workingman's suit.

There were three people at the other table. Two of them were a well-coiffed young man and woman peering intently at a laptop and some papers. The third person was looking at some papers, too, but not intently, and a different kind of papers. He was leaned back perusing a newspaper. There was no bald spot on his silvery, thick head of hair – or maybe it was thick head of toupee – and his black robe somehow looked tailor-made. Although Bonnie could only see him in quarter-profile, she'd seen enough straight-on newspaper and magazine photos of Herschel Greene Q.C. to picture the squared-off face and twinkly blue eyes, hedged by patriarchal grey sideburns down to his square block of a chin. He looked like he should be standing at the wheel of the *Bluenose*, guiding her through the gale.

In Bonnie's pre-interview with the Crown attorney, she'd got the impression that he'd had a few run-ins with Hersh Greene before, and got run over. Seeing the two attorneys in the same room, or at least their backs, reminded her of something the prosecutor had said in that pre-interview. He'd muttered bemusedly, almost to himself, that it was odd there'd been no attempt to plea-bargain: "Not guilty or bust."

A thin, young woman in a long, baggy coat came briskly down the aisle, carrying a yellow Home Hardware plastic bag. She stopped at the gateway in the barrier fence, shrugged off her coat and draped it on the nearest empty chair, disclosing that she was wearing court robes, too. She picked up the yellow plastic bag again, then stepped through the gateway and over to the Crown prosecutor's table. He looked up at her, then down at the bag and nodded and smiled. She sat down beside him and tucked the bag under the table.

Bonnie subtly craned her neck around to see if the bag had flopped open enough to show what was inside. It hadn't. Whatever was in the bag wasn't bigger than a breadbox, though not much smaller, and from the way the thin, young woman had carried it, it wasn't very heavy.

The jury was brought in, and then the prisoner. Jack Burton didn't look like a few months in jail had had much effect on him, except that his hair and beard were trimmed a bit shorter. All rose for the judge, who turned out to be a middle-aged woman with an Acadian first name and a Scots last name. Bonnie found that kind of encouraging, though she couldn't say exactly why.

The day's first witness, called by the Crown, was "Bonnie Darcy Marsden." The full name reminded Bonnie that she and Ben had habitually called her "bonnie Darcy" when she was a baby, and still did, on occasion. Well, Bonnie still did; she had no idea what Ben did on any occasions these days. The Crown prosecutor didn't ask Darcy for much, just to explain that she'd overheard her mother saying over the phone to Jack Burton/Bert Jackson, *"Sure, used to be MacGuigans' Sawmill. But . . . Ben's getting out tomorrow,"* and had secretly told her father about the meeting that had been arranged. Then the Defence got to cross-examine.

Hersh Greene got up and ambled toward Darcy, with the aid of a flathead cane, its handle's rounded ends poking out of his right fist. It didn't look to Bonnie like he had much of a limp; his shoulders stayed straight, and he used the cane in tandem with his right leg, instead of his off-leg like most people who needed a cane would. He put one hand on the rail of the witness box, and the instant Bonnie heard his voice for the first time, her subconscious filing system went: *Hersh Greene = Lorne Greene.* Not exactly the same, of course, but the same kind of deep-chested base that radiated integrity and good will.

What Hersh Greene said was, "Just to clarify for the sake of the jury, Ms. Marsden – well, and my sake as well . . ." From where Bonnie was sitting, she couldn't see Hersh Greene's face, but she was quite sure he'd just flashed Darcy the famous, friendly half-smile from the newspaper pictures. "The reason you told your father that your mother was going to meet with the accused – with Mr. Burton – was because you thought she might be putting herself in danger."

"Yes, sir." Bonnie could see Darcy biting her lip, because her waitress habits had gone and made her call him "sir."

"And what made you think that?"

"Well, Mom had said Dad had said he was scared of the guy. My dad's not the kind of guy that scares easily."

"Tough customer, your dad?"

"Oh, he's really a big moosh, but, um . . ." Bonnie could see Darcy wondering what that question was about, and what might be the wrong answer. "But, a *big* moosh, you know?"

"Well, I guess I'll know soon enough, as will the jury. So, essentially, all that *you* knew about the accused – about Mr. Burton – was what your mother had said your father had said."

"Uh, yeah. Yes."

"Thank you, Ms. Marsden. I have no further questions."

Bonnie was dead sure Hersh Greene was up to something, but she couldn't for the life of her think what. Before she'd had much chance to even try, it was her turn in the hotbox. The Crown prosecutor walked her through essentially the same questions as their pre-interview, and she found herself in the same bind as she had then – except that now she was under oath. The problem was the videotape of Billy Vickers's confession. If it came out that somebody was bootlegging tapes of police interrogations, somebody was going to be in a barrel of trouble. And it was somebody who'd done Bonnie and Ben a very large favour, even if the favour had cost two hundred dollars. As Ben often said, *"There's a difference between what's a crime and what's just against the law."* That unfortunately brought up thoughts of Charlie Warner, but Bonnie pushed them aside to deal with the moment.

How she dealt with it, or tried to, was to say that when Ben's trial was coming up, they'd learned that the reason the excise agents had come after Ben was he'd been named in Billy Vickers's confession. Which was essentially true, and there was no reason — Bonnie hoped — for either the Crown or Hersh Greene to dig up the fact that they couldn't've learned that from Ben's Legal Aid lawyer. The same should hold true about how they'd learned Billy Vickers had also named Jack Burton, which had caused Ben to say, *"Poor dumb kid'd be safer-off in jail."*

Bonnie was sweating piglets until the Crown's questions got safely past those preliminaries and on to 'the night in question.' The Crown entered Melissa's magic pen as evidence — Bonnie had bought her another one the next day — and played the certified, enhanced re-dub an RCMP technician had put on CD. Bonnie could see that the jury was affected by the accused's voice crowing, *"Billy Vickers? Hell, I flambéd the little bastard."* She glanced over at Jack Burton and at Hersh Greene. Neither one of them twitched.

Then the prosecution was done with her and handed her over to the defence. Hersh Greene advanced on her, with his right hand tandeming his cane and his left thumb casually hooked into a pocket of the black vest under his black robe. Bonnie was thrown back to worrying about the videotape, only worse this time. She had no idea of what she was going to say under oath if she got pressed for details on exactly how she'd learned there was a connection between Billy Vickers and Jack Burton. Hersh Greene began with, "If I understand you correctly, Mrs. Marsden . . ."

Smooth. He knew I'd prefer Mrs. and Darcy Ms.

". . . as was the case with your daughter, the only cause you had to imagine my client could be a danger to anyone, was what your husband had said."

"Well, and what Corporal Kowalchuck said."

Hersh Greene cocked his head, like Clyde catching a wind-blown whiff of squirrel. "Corporal Kowalchuck?"

Oh-oh, maybe I shouldn't've said that; maybe get Corporal Kowalchuck in trouble for tales-out-of-school. "Well, I went to see Corporal Kowalchuck because, him being from out west, I thought maybe he'd been the one who'd got my résumé out to Alberta. He wasn't, but since I was there anyway, I mentioned that what happened to Billy Vickers sounded to me like it might not've been an accident."

"Ah. And Corporal Kowalchuck suggested to you that my client may have been responsible."

Bonnie didn't have to be reminded she was under oath. She thought back and heard Corporal Kowalchuck's dry, flat, prairie voice: *'What I might think and what I might prove aren't always the same thing.'* "No, I can say with certainty . . ." *Funny how those businesswoman turns of phrase just slide back on without thinking.* ". . . that all Corporal Kowalchuck said to me about Jack Burton, was that Mr. Burton was someone I should stay away from."

"So, your entire knowledge and opinion of the accused, was based on secondhand and thirdhand rumours. The same kind of exaggerated rumours that led the excise agents to believe your husband to be a major player in the booze and drug trade, instead of just a smalltime criminal."

"No, that's not the same at —"

"I have no further questions for this witness."

Bonnie looked at the judge, who nodded at her and waved her hand at the gateway back to anonymity. Bonnie had barely got through the gate when the judge declared a recess for lunch. Bonnie stood where she was, as everybody else did the All Rise till the judge was gone.

Darcy came scurrying out of their row, carrying Bonnie's coat and excusing her way past people still reaching for theirs. Bonnie bustled up the aisle with her, surprised that Darcy's much younger kidneys couldn't hold out as long as hers. Inevitably, they got slowed down by people coming out of the back rows in front of them. Once out into the lobby, Darcy set up a brisk pace that Bonnie's shorter legs had to struggle to keep up with. Darcy didn't turn off at the sign for the public washrooms, but kept on straight out the front doors. At the top of the front steps, Darcy stopped and called, "Dad!"

Bonnie saw Ben at the bottom of the steps, saw him stop and turn around. Darcy started down the steps toward him, and Bonnie saw no choice but to go along with her. Through Ben's open coat, Bonnie could see that he was wearing the burgundy sweater, and the semi-dress pants she'd found for him at Frenchy's, when the waistband of his weddings-and-funerals suit couldn't be let out any more.

Darcy said, "We're just going to get some lunch, wondered if you'd like to join us?"

Ben said, "Thanks, but I'm, uh, kinda nervous. Wouldn't be very good company. Sorry, but, uh, that's just a fact."

Bonnie believed him. It was hard to see that big, strong man so obviously shaken, and not be able to put her hand on his arm and tell him there was nothing to worry about. But then, it was Ben who'd taken away that possibility.

* * *

Ben found a place to get a burger and a beer, and managed to choke down some of the burger. No way around it, in not many minutes he was going to have to go back into that courtroom again, and the place gave him the willies. Even though he wasn't the one on trial, he knew too well that any judge in a bad mood, or on a whim, could just snap fingers, and you were on your way to jail, or selling your truck to pay the fine. That is, if you couldn't afford a fancy lawyer to weasel you out of it.

And then there was the fact that if the one who *was* on trial today didn't get convicted, if his fancy lawyer found a way to weasel him out of it, Jack Burton would be out on the streets again, and driving the roads of Membertou County.

It didn't help Ben's nerves that Bonnie would be in that courtroom, too. He'd thought about her a lot in the past few weeks, in fact had to work to find things to distract him from thinking about her. But no matter what direction his thinking about Bonnie, and missing her, wandered, he always ran up against the same wall: Charlie Warner sitting in a prison cell. Not that Ben had any deep attachment to Charlie Warner, he hardly knew the guy. But there was no way around the fact that Bonnie didn't seem the least bit sorry for putting him in prison.

Ben managed to get back to the courtroom and sat back down just in time to stand up again when the judge came in. Then, he'd barely got sat down again when "The Crown calls Benjamin Joseph Marsden."

The Crown prosecutor led Ben through his testimony fairly painlessly, not rushing him. Ben was actually starting to get a bit relaxed, when he was turned over to the defence. Ben watched Hersh Greene rise from his chair and come forward: yachtsman's tan, just enough age lines on his face to make him look human, gleaming, black brogues that probably cost more than Ben's truck, silver hair to match his silver tongue. But no, Ben corrected himself on that last thought. From what he'd heard of Mr. Greene's interrogations in the morning, Hersh Greene was far too smooth and clever to sound smooth and silver-tongued. He would always toss in enough hesitations and kitchen table phrases to give the impression there was some just-plain-folks still in his bones.

Just tell the truth, Ben told himself, *except for that part about the videotape. Those kind of guys can't play games with you if you don't play games with them.*

"I understand, Mr. Marsden, that you and your wife are currently, um, estranged?"

Ben was about to say, *We've always been a bit strange,* but decided not. "Yes."

"Might I ask why?"

"You a married man, Mr. Greene?" Hersh Greene looked a

bit miffed, as though he was the only one allowed to ask questions, so Ben went quickly on to, "'Cause if you are, I won't have to explain to you that any marriage has its . . . complications."

There was a chuckle from the direction of the jury box. Hersh Greene ducked his head and smiled. "Touché. 'Nuff said. Now, Mr. Marsden, you said in your testimony that on the night in question, you came up behind the accused – my client – and applied a choke hold. Would you please explain to the jury what a choke hold is?"

Ben turned toward the jury box, a polyglot amalgam of ages, sexes and colours. Those eyes and faces trained on him, and the ones he could feel from the rest of the courtroom, put on a choke hold of their own. He heard the long-ago voice of a high school girlfriend, when he'd been paranoid-frozen about an exam they were going in to write, *'Just take your time, Ben – you know the answers.'* Unfortunately, the voice was Bonnie's. "Uh . . . Well, a choke hold is . . . you got two arteries running up the sides of your throat – carotid arteries, or caratoid or something – you can feel them best just under the back of your jaw. Those arteries carry the blood supply to your brain. If they get choked off, it don't take very long before you pass out."

Hersh Greene said, "So you've had, um . . . *extensive* medical training, Mr. Marsden?"

"Not hardly. Oh, I had to take some training to be a first responder with the fire department. But I knew about choke holds long before then. Way back years ago I used to pick up a few bucks working weekends as a doorman."

"A doorman?"

"In a tavern. The Black Briar, in Raddallton."

"Ah. You mean a bar bouncer."

"Well, yeah – doorman, bouncer."

The silvery head nodded thoughtfully at that. "Are you aware, Mr. Marsden, why even trained police officers are very reluctant to use choke holds?"

"Well, yeah – you gotta be careful, 'cause if you cut the blood supply off too long, you can cause brain damage."

"Yes, permanent brain damage. Or even death." Hersh Greene hooked a thumb in his vest pocket, leaned on his cane, and looked mistily off at some point over the heads of the jury, as though he was contemplating something. "Did you enjoy your forty days in provincial jail, Mr. Marsden?"

"Not hardly."

"It must've seemed more than unfair to you, that you were stuck in jail while Mr. Burton – a man you knew by *rumour* to be a much bigger criminal than you – was walking around free."

Ben shook his head. "Didn't have nothing to do with me. As I said all along, I hardly knew the guy, and didn't wanna have anything to do with him."

"Perhaps that was true, at first. But after forty days to brood on it . . . And then, the day you got out of prison, you learned from your daughter that your wife was going to meet Mr. Burton that night. You snuck over to the meeting place and lurked in the woods. Mrs. Marsden, operating on the basis of *rumours* you'd circulated about Mr. Burton, assumed in all sincerity that my client had murdered Billy Vickers. She thought to trick the accused into a confession.

"Mr. Burton responded to your wife's question with a joke about the unfortunate young man's accident – admittedly a twisted joke in poor taste, but if that was a crime, Monty Python would've been locked up long ago. When my client saw that Mrs. Marsden had made an odd motion with the odd-looking pen, as though she'd flicked a switch that was surreptitiously recording him, he reacted angrily, as most people would.

"And you saw your chance – the perfect opportunity to have your revenge and come off looking like a hero. You snuck out of the woods, to come up on Mr. Burton from behind . . ." Hersh Greene hooked his cane over the railing, stretched his arms out in front of him and took a few sort of Boris Karloff steps forward, then clenched his hands around an imaginary neck. "And, exerting the full extent of your strength, not being careful at all, attempted to squeeze the life out of Jack Burton. It didn't matter to you whether he died of brain-blood deprivation, or of strangulation, just as long as he died.

"I put it to you, Mr. Marsden, that you intended to murder this man who currently stands accused of murder. In fact, you thought you *had* succeeded in murdering him. When his body went limp, your *extensive* medical knowledge of choke holds and strangulation told you he was dead. But, after you'd dropped him to the ground, and then discovered he was still breathing, you had to concoct this story to your wife – and to the police – that you were only intending to subdue Mr. Burton to protect her. And now you are continuing to carry through with that fabrication, to the point of testifying against an innocent man accused of murder.

"Isn't *that* – what I've just described – what actually happened on MacGuigan Road the night you were released from prison?"

It seemed to Ben that the courtroom was tilting like a pinball arcade. Hersh Greene couldn't've caught him more offguard if he'd pulled a gun out of his vest and shot him. When Ben opened his mouth to say that wasn't what happened at all, his tongue was all twisted up. Before he could get it untwisted, Hersh Greene said, "No further questions," and turned away.

* * *

Bonnie saw Hersh Greene turn away from the witness box and head back to his chair, saw Ben groping for words and breath, and she saw what Herschel Greene Q.C. had been up to. With a charge as serious as first-degree murder, all he had to do was plant a "reasonable doubt" in the minds of the jury, and they wouldn't convict.

As the defence attorney was sitting down, the Crown prosecutor was standing up and saying, "Redirect, Your Honour. I do have one further question for the witness, arising directly out of my learned friend's cross-examination."

"Proceed."

The prosecutor stooped down to pick up the yellow Home

Hardware bag and took out a length of black stovepipe, maybe a foot long. "This is a standard piece of heavy-gauge metal stovepipe, seven inches in diameter –"

The defence objected that this was a court of law, not a yard sale, but it seemed to Bonnie that Hersh Greene didn't really have strong objections to the Crown prosecutor making a fool of himself. The Crown assured the judge that this was utterly relevant to the case, and pertaining directly to the defence's cross-examination. The judge said, "It had better be. Proceed."

The Crown prosecutor did seem bent on making a fool of himself: entering the sales slip as evidence the piece of stove pipe had been bought just that morning, and handing the pipe to the foreman of the jury so he could see it hadn't been tampered with, except for the seam being rivetted together at point of purchase. The foreman, who looked to Bonnie to be an early-retired businessman, looked the pipe over, turned it around in his hands, shrugged okay and handed it back. The prosecutor carried it back toward the witness box and said, "Please stand up, Mr. Marsden, and hold your arms out in front of you." Then he held the piece of stove pipe up vertically between Ben's hands. "Now, please wrap your hands around the stove pipe, if you would."

As Ben did, the corner of Bonnie's eye caught a movement in the jury box, only a small movement, but sudden. When she looked in that direction, she saw the foreman's head settling forward on his neck again, after jerking back in surprise. Most people didn't realize just how big Big Ben Marsden's hands were, until they saw them handling something they'd handled themselves.

The Crown prosecutor said, "Now, Mr. Marsden, would you please squeeze the pipe with both hands, with . . . um, what was the phrase my learned friend used . . . ? 'Exerting the full extent of your strength.'" Ben looked uncertainly at the Crown prosecutor. The Crown prosecutor nodded, "Give 'er."

Bonnie saw Ben's hands tightening, the knuckles whitening. His lips drew back from his clenched teeth, but not in the same expression she'd seen over Jack Burton's shoulder that night.

Then he'd been concentrated on applying just the right amount of pressure in the right places; now he was just concentrated on 'givin' 'er.'

Bonnie knew what was going to happen before it did. There was a crunching, crumpling sound, and the straight tube of heavy-gauge metal stovepipe turned into something more like an hourglass.

In the slack-jawed silence that followed, Bonnie heard a small sound. It might've been a muffled cough, or a suppressed bark, or – to someone who'd had previous conversations with Jack Burton – a laugh. Bonnie looked toward the prisoner. He was looking at Ben, with the last kind of expression Bonnie would've expected from someone whose first line of defence had just been drop-kicked out the window. It was something sort of like a smile. It occurred to Bonnie that the only thing she'd ever heard Jack Burton say that didn't have a twist or a hook or a trapdoor in it was, "Your husband's a stand-up guy, Bonnie Marsden."

The seats Bonnie and Darcy had found when they came back from lunch were on the aisle, even though Bonnie hardly needed an aisle seat for leg room. As Ben walked back toward his own seat, Bonnie bent her aisle-side elbow to bring her hand up beside her shoulder. As Ben went by, his hand brushed across hers and gave it the tiniest hint of a squeeze.

Bonnie knew she should be feeling happy and relieved that the biggest shark in local, legal waters hadn't pulled off his plan to free Jack Burton by trashing Ben. And she was, but she was feeling something else as well. When she looked across the fence at the judge murmuring with the court clerk about some detail, at Hersh Greene scratching his eyebrow like, *Oh well, it was worth a try,* at the Crown prosecutor and his assistant practically high-fiving each other, at the jury penciling into their notebook-score-cards, what passed through Bonnie's mind was: *It all comes down to this? Queen's Knight to King Four? Straight Flush beats a Full House?*

10

Bonnie came home from cleaning a recently divorced man's home and found a message on her answering machine to call Corporal Kowalchuck. When she did, the receptionist said he was out on patrol, but the dispatcher would get the message to him and he'd likely call back on his cell phone. Not many minutes later, her phone rang. "Hello?"

"Mrs. Marsden, it's Corporal Kowalchuck. I thought you'd like to know as soon as possible – well, it'll be in the papers tomorrow, but they'll likely get it muddled. The jury returned its verdict on Jack Burton today. Guilty."

"Oh, thank God." Bonnie's two experiences with courtrooms in the last six months had convinced her that nothing was guaranteed.

"The judge didn't waste any time passing sentence: first-degree murder is an automatic life sentence with no chance of parole for twenty-five years. But it's not over yet. His lawyer is bound to file an appeal on some grounds or other. I'll keep you posted."

"Thank you."

"No, thank *you*. If it wasn't for you, he'd still be at large. Bye now."

A few days later, Corporal Kowalchuck called back and said, "It's, um, very strange. Mr. Burton hasn't filed an appeal. In fact, he's being processed right now for transportation. He's being moved to Kingston Penitentiary in Ontario, away from known associates. It certainly wouldn't've been Mr. Greene's decision not to appeal – the longer the litigation, the longer the bill."

"Well, you said before, Corporal, you wouldn't presume to understand the way Jack Burton thinks, or want to."

"That is true. Well, as things stand, the case is closed and Jack Burton is in prison. So maybe that's the end of it."

That 'maybe' stuck in Bonnie's mind, and niggled at her from time to time. But, since she couldn't think of any possible "maybe" about it, and time didn't stop counting out bits of change for her to deal with . . . Melissa was learning to read, and that meant learning to help her with her homework reading without helping her too much to learn. The snow was melting again, this time probably for good, and slow enough that the run-off seeped gradually down along the still-frozen ground. That meant a change of boots and coat and other clothes for Melissa, from the ones she'd worn through the winter and the ones she'd outgrown since last spring. And it meant a change in the cleaning gear Bonnie packed into her car most mornings, to deal with the muddy snow-melt inside outside doors.

One thing that didn't change was the situation with Ben, or non-situation. Bonnie sat up some nights smoking cigarettes, wondering what she could or should do to change things, adding and subtracting the same things: Ben had no right to judge her, after he'd brought trouble into their home with his moonshine liquor; but then, he'd probably saved her life when Jack Burton caught onto her so-clever trick; then again, who owed who what? The inventory went back thirty years. A lot of water under the bridge, as said the captain of the *Titanic*.

One thing she was sure of was that Charlie Warner wasn't going to have as tough a time in prison as the average, smallish, middle-aged man thrown in with a bunch of hardened criminals. Someone who knew as much about firearms as he did? They'd be falling all over each other trying to be nice to him and get a chance to chat with him.

Moyle, Robbie and Darcy had fallen back into the same habits as when Ben was in jail. Moyle called from Alberta every few days, Robbie came home on weekends, and Darcy on her waitress-weekends. Eventually Bonnie had to tell them they didn't have to come home for *all* their weekends, if they were ever going to have lives of their own. On one clear, sunny waitress-weekend, when the bus from the city to Raddallton had no excuse to run late, it of course did, and Bonnie had to boot it to get her and Darcy home before the schoolbus. They got to the schoolbus stop a few minutes early, and while they sat waiting, Darcy said, "So, um, you seen Dad lately?"

"Nope."

"Oh. You know if he's still living where he was?"

"Far as I know."

"Well, if he's just staying out at a friend's hunting camp, it doesn't sound like he's going very far for long – like maybe he just has to think over whatever he has to think over."

"Maybe."

It seemed like Darcy was going to say something more, but then the schoolbus was there, and Darcy was hunkering her seat forward and opening her door so Melissa could squeeze into the back. Melissa was all eager to take Clyde for a walk in the woods, now that the snow finally wasn't too deep.

Bonnie said, "Okay, honey, but be careful crossing the bridge, it'll be slippy." The "bridge" was the dam Ben had built out of scrap sheet metal, rocks, earth, tar and old railroad ties, to turn their creek-swamp into a trout pond.

As Bonnie and Darcy went on into the house, Darcy carrying Melissa's schoolbag, Darcy said, "You never let me go off into our back woods by myself till I was a lot older."

"Oh, she can't get too far lost. Last year the Dunnigans put in a logging road right along the back of our property line. And Clyde'll stick close to her. Like your father says, we only get otic dogs."

"Otic dogs?"

"Yeah – Floyd was psych-otic and Clyde's neur-otic." Bonnie

immediately regretted bringing in Ben's eccentric sense of humour, and even more so that she'd said 'says,' as in the present tense. She moved to the stove and counter to start making tea and cutting up an apple and cheese for when Melissa got back.

"Do you think, Mom, um, maybe if you talked to Dad, told him maybe you feel bad about –"

"Goddammit, Charlie Warner had enough guns and ammunition in his basement to start a war! So what if it wasn't one of his guns that killed that boy – this time. Kids have been known to break into houses, looking for whatever they can find." Bonnie realized she was almost yelling, and not almost flailing her paring knife in the air. "Oh, I'm sorry, dear, I'm not mad at *you*."

"I know, Mom."

Bonnie was too flustered to warm the teapot properly, just threw in three teabags and poured boiled water in on top of them. Darcy had already got down the teacups. Or tea mugs, rather – Ben's great-grandmother's teacups rarely came out of the cupboard, except for dusting. Bonnie said, "I know it sounds like kind of a foolish little argument to make your father and I not be living together. But, I guess it's just, sort of a symptom. He sees things one way, and I see them another." She looked down at the tabletop and muttered, "So different there isn't even an argument."

"Are you guys going to get a . . .?" Darcy couldn't seem to say the word she was headed for. "You know, something legal?"

"I don't know." Bonnie reached for the steeped teapot, and for a way to change the subject. "Say, you probably didn't hear about it in the city, but we had a break-in at the firehall week before last."

"Somebody robbed a volunteer fire department?"

"Yeah. But the only thing they took was the machine that drives the Jaws of Life."

"Huh?"

"That's exactly what everybody said, until they started thinking about what kind of machine it is. Seems it's a hydraulic to drive a sort of giant chisel to punch through car walls." Bonnie held her right hand out like a judo chopper, and drove it forward and back. "Kind of like an overpowered wood-splitter. So, someone running a backwoods firewood operation . . . Whoever took it better hope they don't get caught by anybody from around here – stealing from the volunteer fire department."

"Maybe they figured the insurance would cover it."

"It will – minus twelve hundred deductible. That's a lot of bake sales and flea markets and supper dances. If the Ladies' Auxiliary ever gets their hands on those guys . . ."

Darcy nodded and laughed. But then Clyde's frantic barking cut in from outside, and Melissa's voice shouting, "Mommy! Darcy!"

Bonnie got to the back door before Darcy. Melissa was running up the hill. Clyde was running ahead of her, then running back to her, then running ahead again. When Melissa saw Bonnie and Darcy in the doorway, she shouted, "Somebody's stealing our trees!"

Darcy muttered, *"What?"*

Bonnie stepped out of the doorway, calling, "What's the matter, honey?"

Melissa slowed down and panted out, "Me and Clyde walked back almost to the new road, and there's two big trees cut down on our property!"

Bonnie and Darcy looked at each other, then reached for their coats. On the other side of the trout pond was the Marsdens' woodlot, which Bonnie sometimes thought too grand a name for a few acres of overgrown hillside. But the going wasn't too rough, since Ben habitually whiled away a few winter days chainsawing out the worst tangles. Nonetheless, Bonnie was starting to feel a bit winded, when Melissa said, "Not much more farther. I wasn't gonna come this far, but Clyde started barking loud and ran aheada me. There, see?"

Bonnie saw. Two good-sized trees had been taken down, taking smaller ones with them. All that was left of one was a jumble of amputated limbs around where the trunk had been hauled away. The other one had only been limbed enough to get a chainsaw at the trunk, which had been sliced through two or three times after felling, and then left lying there. Bonnie murmured, "What a sin."

Darcy said, "Those trees must've been at least fifty years old."

"I don't get it. Why would someone fell two trees, cut one up and haul it away, and the other one just make a few cuts in and leave it?"

Melissa put in, "They're *our* trees!"

Darcy said, "Maybe they ran out of daylight, and decided to come back and get the other logs the next day."

"No, this wasn't done yesterday, or the day before." Bonnie pointed at the ground around the wreckage. "The footprints are just smudge-marks in the snow. Things haven't been melting fast enough to do that in just a couple of days. And," she pointed at the butchered trunk, "instead of working their way along that, cutting it into haulable logs, they just cut through it once about ten feet along, then once more further up, and then left it alone."

Darcy murmured, "I wonder . . . Maybe . . ." and crouched down to peer at the remains.

"Maybe what?"

"Well, both these trees are maples – or *were* maples."

With no leaves, Bonnie couldn't tell if they were maple or oak or something else, but she took Darcy's word for it. Part-time in high school and full-time for a while after, Darcy'd been more or less apprentice to a local cabinetmaker named Donald Fisher. She likely would've eventually taken over the business, and not moved to Halifax, if Mr. Fisher hadn't taken a heart attack and aborted "eventually." Bonnie said, "So . . .?"

"When I was working with old Donald restoring furniture, there were a couple of pieces that were bird's-eye maple, and it was a bitch – I mean it was difficult –"

Melissa crowed, "I heard you!"

" – because bird's-eye maple is so rare and so expensive. I mean, if this tree'd be worth two hundred dollars to a sawmill, if it was bird's-eye it'd be more like a thousand."

Bonnie goggled. "*A thousand dollars?*"

"More or less. Bird's-eye's like bumblebees."

Bonnie said, "Huh?"

Melissa said, "The birds and bees?"

Darcy said, "Like bumblebees 'cause bumblebees can't fly – I mean, according to aeronautic science. Well, science can't tell you what makes the grain of a bird's-eye maple do all that neat stuff, maybe a virus or fungus or something else, they've never been able to figure it out. So, same thing as bumblebees, if bird's-eye's got no scientific reason to happen, it can't happen, right? But it happens.

"But, the thing is, you can't tell from the outside of a maple tree if it's bird's-eye or not. Donald said if you're real careful and know what you're doing, you can strip off a bit of bark and see. But if you don't know what you're doing – the fastest way to tell is cut it down and cut it open."

"*Kill* the tree just to find out if it's worth stealing?"

Darcy said disgustedly, "Yeah."

Bonnie looked up, trying to gauge how tall those trees would've been, in comparison to the ones around them. Definitely tall enough to be seen from the Dunnigans' logging road. She said, seething, "Let's get back to the house, and I'll give Morton Dunnigan a call before supper."

There were a lot of Dunnigans in the phone book, but Bonnie knew that ever since Morton Sr. died, sixty-year-old Junior was the head of the clan. When she'd told him about the maple trees, trying not to sound like she'd tried and convicted him already, he said, "Us Dunnigans been working the woods for five generations, and we don't go in for poaching anymore'n we go in for being poached."

"Well, maybe you, or one of the other guys, saw somebody else back there?"

"I'll ask 'em when I sees 'em. But me, I aren't seen anybody on our road except us Dunnigans. Oh, excepting last week or thereabouts, there was a pickup snugged in close to where you're talking about. I had to squeeze my truck past careful, to keep the paint on. But I didn't think nothing of it, 'cause it was Ben's truck."

That hit Bonnie a thump. "You're sure it was Ben's truck?"

"Sure for sure."

Bonnie couldn't doubt it. There were a lot of old red pickup trucks around Membertou County, but Ben's was hard to mistake. A couple of years ago, when the driver's door got too rusted out to patch, Ben had found a primer-black door at a wrecker's and hadn't yet got around to finding the right shade of red paint to match the rest. Bonnie forced her voice to stay polite for, "Well, thanks for keeping an eye out, Morton. Bye now." But as soon as she'd hung up, out burst, "*Bastard!*"

Melissa scolded, "Mommy!" Bonnie nodded that she would remember to put a quarter in the swear jar, and clicked the microwave to finish heating up the gravy for hot chicken sandwiches.

Darcy said, "Who – Morton Dunnigan?"

"No – he said he didn't know anything about anybody taking trees off our property, and I believe him. But, he said last week he saw a pickup truck snugged in tight at the back of our woods. Your father's truck."

"Dad wouldn't –"

"I don't know anymore what your father would or wouldn't do. Two months ago I would've said he wouldn't walk out on us."

Melissa said, "He meets me after school sometimes."

The microwave beeped and fortunately moved things on to dishing up supper. After chewing on her first few bites, and a few other things, Bonnie said to Darcy, "There's no phone at Jake MacGuigan's hunting camp, so I'll drive up there after supper. Would you come along? So it's kind of a family situation, instead of just him and me?"

"Sure."

Bonnie wasn't intimately familiar with Jake MacGuigan's hunting camp, but had an idea of where it was. There were a few houses along that gravel road, and then a long stretch of nothing but woods. Around where Bonnie thought the place might be, there were three pickup trucks parked by the side of the road. Bonnie had been expecting only one. And the trucks there meant that the driveway up to the cabin hadn't been plowed. Or maybe there was no driveway, and they just brought in anything too heavy to carry by ATV.

Bonnie pulled in behind the trucks and turned off the ignition, but not all the way to Off. She left the radio on, switched the dome light on, and said to Melissa in the back seat, "We won't be long, but stay in the car and do your homework, okay?"

"Okay."

"If you get scared or something, just lean on the horn."

"I won't get scared."

As Bonnie and Darcy climbed out, Bonnie switched on the flashlight she kept in the glove compartment, and played it along the edge of the woods till she found the mouth of a path. The path turned out to be mostly gravel, with only a few thin patches of snow, had a bit of an upward slope to it, and was wide enough to walk side-by-side. After not many steps, Bonnie could see a flickering glow up ahead. A few steps farther, and she could hear the crackle of a bonfire, and the sound of lubricated male voices – not yelling-drunk, just loose and lazy.

Bonnie knew immediately what was going on. It wasn't at all unusual for men to spend a winter day chainsawing brush and deadfalls, and come nightfall burn up all that was too twisted, thin or rotted for the woodstove. It also wasn't unusual for the bonfire to include things like household trash and old tires. Which wasn't legal anymore, but it was hard to change the habits of generations. Especially for people who suddenly found themselves ordered to sort their garbage, and to drive forty miles to the nearest landfill site, where they had to pay by the pound for everything they dumped. Bonnie didn't exactly approve of burning tires and trash, but she knew she wasn't exactly likely to load up a truck and drive it to the dump herself. And burning was at least better than dumping it in the woods.

Bonnie half-whispered to Darcy, "Try and walk softly, till we get close enough to hear what they're talking about." From then on, Bonnie kept the flashlight beam trained down at the ground in front of them. As they neared the top of the slope, Bonnie turned off the flashlight and touched Darcy on the arm to stop.

Now that they were close enough to make out words, the first voice Bonnie heard was definitely Shaky Jake MacGuigan's. Jake's speaking voice sounded like he looked: reedy, thin and prematurely aged. He'd got the nickname because his voice and his hands had such a permanent tremble, you'd swear he was coming off a three-day drunk, if you didn't know he'd already been like that when the strongest thing he drank was milk. Unlike the rest of the MacGuigans, Shaky Jake seemed like a wisp of wind would carry him away, or break his fragile bones. But he worked full days in the gas station's service bay, and Bonnie had seen him toss around tractor tires as tall as she was. At the moment, what Shaky Jake MacGuigan's desiccated voice had to say was, "Gordie Howe."

A middle-aged male voice Bonnie didn't recognize said, "Bobby Hull."

Shaky Jake said, "Nah – one trick pony."

Ben's voice rumbled in, "Good trick, but . . ."

The voice Bonnie didn't recognize said, "Bobby Orr, then."

Jake said, "That's worth arguing."

A very young man's voice said, "Wayne Gretzky."

Jake MacGuigan said, "Nah, Gretzky doesn't count."

The unknown middle-aged male said, apparently to the young one, "You see, son, by the time Gretzky got into the big leagues, there were eight hundred teams and eight gazillion players, and it was all so watered-down there's just no way to say what he might've or mightn't've done with real competition."

"Oh."

Ben's voice came back in, "You can argue Gordie Howe and Bobby Orr and all them till the cows come home – thinking in terms of statistics and longevity of career and all that. But think of it this way. You're coaching the seventh game of the Stanley

Cup, two minutes to go and you're down by a goal. Who do you put on the ice?"

Jake MacGuigan said, "Well, sure, Ben, if you put it that way there's nothing to argue about."

The unfamiliar middle-aged man said, and Bonnie could hear the shrug in his voice, "Cut and dried."

The young voice said, "Huh?"

By then, Bonnie had decided that she wasn't going to overhear anything about maple trees, climbed the last of the slope and stepped out of the woods. Four male faces turned toward her and Darcy. The four were sitting on lawn chairs a few feet back from the fire, each with a beer in his hand. Nearest to Bonnie was wizened Jake MacGuigan, and Big Ben Marsden the farthest away. Shaky Jake said with attempted casualness, "Oh hi, Bonnie." He turned his head slightly aside for, "Lester, this is Ben's wife Bonnie," then looked back at her and pointed his thumb at the plumpish, middle-aged man and thin young man sitting beside him. "Lester Perkins and his young fella."

Bonnie said, formulaically politely, "My daughter Darcy."

Darcy said, "Hi."

Ben said nothing.

After a moment of no sound but the hiss and snap of the fire, Jake MacGuigan said, "Yeah, well, poor Ben thought he'd have the place to himself, but now I'm bunking in with him up here at camp for a while – guess you heard why."

Bonnie said flatly, "No."

Shaky Jake MacGuigan shrugged, kind of ruefully humorous, "Jeez, I would've thought she'd have it all over the county by now."

Lester Perkins put in, "Tell-a-graph, tell-a-phone –"

Shaky Jake allowed as how, "I wouldn't keep it to myself if I was her."

It had never occurred to Bonnie before, and she was surprised it hadn't, that Jake MacGuigan looked like a dry-roasted chicken wing with a mustache.

"Ya see," Shaky Jake went on, "couple Fridays ago, when I

got home from work, the wife had kindly packed up a couple days' gear for me – 'cause now as the rivers are thawed clear, me and a couple of other guys were going way back in the woods to spend the weekend fly-fishing. Good for my health and easy on the budget."

"Easy to lose it," came from Lester.

"I had some money squirrelled away, and where we was really headed was into the city –"

Lester put in, "For that big trout pond in Halifax."

" – where we rented a couple motel rooms, and spent the weekend playing the casino and partying. The only damper on the weekend was my danged wife forgot to pack me extra socks, so I had to rinse out my one pair in the bathtub every night and hope they'd be dry by morning. Other'n that, just a crazy-ass weekend and no harm done to anybody. I even thought to pick up a couple of farmed trout at the fishmarket to bring home."

"You don't miss a trick," Lester contributed.

"Yeah, I'm a goddamn genius. So, I gets home on the Sunday night and the wife asks me how it went and I says, 'Just fine, except I spent the weekend tramping the woods with cold, wet feet – you forgot to pack me extra socks!' And the wife says, 'I put them in your tackle box.'"

Lester cackled with laughter and sputtered, "Every time I hear that, it cracks me up!"

Bonnie didn't laugh.

"So," Jake MacGuigan shrugged his scanty eyebrows at her, "I figured I'd maybe better camp out at camp for a few days. Sometimes, you know, the best thing is to just sit out a little time in the penalty box – let things cool down." He took another slurp of his beer, looked around, then stood up. "Well, it's turning chilly out here, time I went inside."

Lester Perkins stood up, too. "Yeah, time I got this young fella home before it's past his bedtime. See ya."

When the three extraneous males were gone, Darcy said, "Jeez, after all that tea with supper and then bouncing around in the car, I'd better go take a walk in the woods," and headed off without asking for the flashlight.

Now that there was only Bonnie and Ben and the fire, Ben finally spoke. "I wasn't one of the fellas that went partying with –"

"I don't care! How much did you get for the tree?"

"Huh?"

"Melissa took Clyde for a walk in our woods this afternoon and found the trees."

"Well, I guess she would, walking in the woods."

"The trees you cut down!"

"I haven't cut down any trees except what I thinned out last winter for firewood."

"Don't lie to me, Ben. Darcy figured out why there were two big maple trees cut down and only one hauled away – because the other one turned out not to be a bird's-eye."

"What? Somebody killed an old tree just to see if it was worth extra money?"

"*Somebody?* Morton Dunnigan saw *your* truck parked back there on his logging road."

"Well, then he saw another truck that looked like mine. I ain't driv down that road but the once, when the Dunnigans first put it through, just for curiosity." Ben looked away from her and into the fire. He was hard to read, with the flamelight dancing over his face. "I don't know if I'm madder at whoever did it, or at you for thinking it was me."

Bonnie wavered. If he was telling the truth, she'd really put her foot in it this time. "Darcy said a bird's-eye maple could be worth a thousand dollars."

"Well, that might tempt me – but I'd get somebody that knew how to tell bird's-eye without cutting it down. And I sure as hell wouldn't go ahead and do it without talking to you. That's *our* property."

Bonnie was getting a lot of confusing signals. Not just from getting her anger and certainty undermined, but from talking so intently with someone who was partly the man she'd talked to just about every day for thirty years or so, and partly a stranger.

One thing that was certain, though, was, "There's not a lot of trucks around that look like yours."

"Maybe just passing by at a glance . . ."

From what Morton Dunnigan had said, it wasn't a passing glance. He'd been very aware of the vehicle he was trying to squeeze past without mingling paint jobs. "Have you been loaning your truck to anybody lately?"

"Not really loaning, sort of time-sharing. When I'm filling-in at the gas station, or Jake or me's got other work on, we take my truck one day and his vehicle the next. There's nobody like somebody who runs a gas station for being sensitive about the cost of gas."

"So, Jake MacGuigan might drop you off somewhere and have your truck for the day."

"The trees couldn't've been Jake – he wouldn't do a thing like that."

Bonnie wasn't so sure what Jake MacGuigan might or might not do, especially after the story of his 'fishing weekend.' Shaky Jake might not be as rough and nefarious as the rest of the Mac-Guigans, but he was still a MacGuigan.

"But, ya know," Ben added on, as though something had just occurred to him, "days I go in Jake's vehicle, my truck's just sitting up here, with the key under the mat. Never thought twice about it, not many people drive this far up this road."

Something occurred to Bonnie as well. "Funny that somebody should be going around stealing trees not long after the Jaws-of-Life machine got stolen for probably a wood-splitter."

"You wouldn't use a wood-splitter on lumber you were planning to sell to furniture makers."

"It still seems like a funny coincidence."

Ben suddenly laughed. "There *is* one funny thing about that machine – that I know and the Chief knows and a couple of other guys at the firehall know, but whoever stole it surely didn't know. It has to have some special kind of hydraulic-lubricating oil, that you can only get from the company that manufactures the machine. So, sooner or later either whoever stole it is going to be stupid enough to try and order from the factory and have to give the serial number, or stupid enough to fill it up with plain 10W30 and the damn thing'll seize up good."

Bonnie laughed with him. And she did feel with him again; all the horrible complexities of the past weeks had stepped out of the way. She said, "There's an even funnier possibility."

"What's that?"

Bonnie opened her mouth to tell him, but another voice came out from behind her. It was Melissa, gleefully shouting, "Daddy!" and running out of the path through the woods.

Bonnie stepped in front of her and bit out, "I told you to stay in the car!"

"But I finished my homework!"

"You promised to stay in the car!" Bonnie took hold of Melissa's arm and started for the path. "Come on!"

"But —"

"Go with your mother, pumpkin," Ben's voice called from behind them, sounding like his throat was tight. "I'll take you for a burger on Friday."

As Bonnie charged down the path with Melissa in tow, she called out, "Darcy!"

"I'm coming!" came from somewhere behind and off to the side.

* * *

Ben watched his wife and little daughter disappear out of range of the firelight. Then he turned his head to look into the fire, and hunkered forward in his chair. A movement caught the corner of his eye. He looked in that direction and saw his other daughter coming towards him. She stopped beside the nearest empty lawn chair, but didn't sit down. She said, "So, how're you doing, Dad?"

"Oh . . . I'm doin'. You?"

"Fine. Mom says you got some part-time work at MacGuigans' garage."

"Yeah. I'm better at wood than machinery, but I can pump gas and change oil."

Darcy looked away from him and towards the path down to the road, where her mother and sister would be waiting for her. Then she looked back at him and said, "Don't you think you and Mom should . . . talk?"

"We just did."

"I mean about why you're living out here like Huckleberry Finn."

"We *did* talk about that, when it happened." He fished a chunk of brush out of the pile behind his chair and chucked it on the fire. "I haven't been able to think of anything else to say about it since then. Maybe your mother will eventually."

"But, doesn't it seem like kind of a silly little thing for you and Mom to be, um . . ."

"Silly little thing? Is that what your mother calls it? Charlie Warner – who never hurt a flea, and kept his hobby guns locked up like Fort Knox – is going to be locked up in a federal penitentiary with murderers and rapists. When he should be easing into the retirement he worked hard for all his life, puttering away inventing things. All because he was fool enough to let Bonnie's Cleaning Service into his home. What kind of a person could do something like that to a harmless old duffer – and *still* think it was the right thing to do?"

"What kind of a person could walk out on his family?"

"You think I *want* to be here, instead of waking up to breakfast with your mother and Melissa – and you when you're home for a visit?"

Darcy's pretty face twisted into something like a smirk, complicated by tears. "When was the last time I was awake for breakfast?"

"Yeah, I shoulda said dinner." He slipped his eyes off her. Funny how it was easier to talk to somebody when you were looking at the fire instead of them. "Sitting out here in the woods, staring into the fire, or the one in there," Ben twitched his head in the direction of the cabin, where some MacGuigan of an earlier generation had decided that all the rocks lying around should make for a fieldstone fireplace, "I keep revolving back to the minute I walked out the door, trying to see a way I could've or should've done something different."

"Keep trying, okay?"

"I can't seem to stop." He took another sip of his almost-gone beer, warm from the fire and his hand. "I don't want you to take my side, Darce, or anybody's side. This is between me and your mother."

"Well, I better get going."

After Darcy was gone, Ben got up and tossed a few clumps of amputated alders onto the fire. With houses or camps in the woods, if you didn't keep the undergrowth down so some breeze could get through, the place would be vicious with blackflies and mosquitoes. Shaky Jake came back out with another couple of beers and they sat watching the fire, not saying much. After awhile of just the fire talking, Jake said with some gravity, "Ya know, I ain't exactly a expert on marriage, except in learning from my mistakes, sometimes. But I do know one thing that's essential, for keeping a marriage together and operational."

Ben said, "What's that?" in an *I'll bite* kind of way.

"Every now and then you gotta just haul back and give it to her."

Ben blinked at the fire, then at Shaky Jake. *"What?"*

"Oh, I know it sounds bad, but it's just a plain fact. Every now and then you gotta just haul back and give it to her. Give her the last word, give her the decision, nod your head and let it lie. Often as not, she'll ponder on it and say all the things to herself you was gonna say. Or even, sometimes – hard to believe, I know – sometimes if you give her the last word, you'll ponder on it and come around to thinking she was right."

Ben laughed, but it came out more of a grunt. "Oh, I know that one, Shaky. Me and Bonnie'd never've lasted's long's we did, if I hadn't learned to bite the bullet and go for a walk in the woods, but this, uh, this current situation, it's, uh, a bit more complicated than that."

"Yeah?"

Ben was tempted to tell him. So far, Ben hadn't said a word to anybody outside the family, about Bonnie and Charlie Warner. If word did get out, it was the kind of thing Bonnie would have to carry for the rest of her life. People in Membertou County had long memories, and people anywhere liked the convenience of being able to define someone by one act, to know at first sight and for all time whether this or that person should be admired or despised. Bonnie obviously hadn't gone around bragging that she'd put Charlie Warner away. And keeping it to herself wasn't because she was ashamed of it: she wasn't ashamed that she'd nudged the police into looking closer at Rose Coffin's now ex-husband, but still nobody knew about that except herself and Ben and Corporal Kowalchuck, and maybe-probably Rose. It had seemed to Ben that if Bonnie hadn't wanted that known – that and a few other things along the same lines – it wasn't his prerogative to make it known. Still, it was a great temptation to tell Jake MacGuigan exactly why he was camped out at the MacGuigans' hunting camp, and have Shaky Jake's certain sympathy and approval. No doubt, soon after he'd told Jake, all of the MacGuigans and half of Membertou County would be choosing up sides in the Marsden family quarrel. It was too rare and weird a secret to expect anybody to keep – anybody who wasn't blood, or bloodless.

While thinking that through, Ben had got up and tossed the last few pieces of an old plastic lawn chair onto the fire, along with a few tarry chunks of rotted railway tie. When he sat back down again and picked up his half-gone beer, all he said in reply to Jake's question mark was, "It's kinda complicated."

Shaky Jake didn't push it, and after awhile started yawning and went back inside. Ben sat up, waiting for the fire to die.

The next day, Ben didn't have any paying work on and wasn't needed to fill in at the garage. So he set up a couple of sawhorses in the yard and set to work paying off some of his informal rent. Some of the floorboards in the cabin were getting warped and splintery – probably put on green way back when, by someone who was better at machinery than wood. Partway through the morning, Lester Perkins came up the path and said cheerfully, "I think I mighta dropped my lighter here last night, probably where I was sitting by the firepit. The wife gave me a Zippo for my birthday, and she'll be some pissed if I lost it already."

"I aren't seen it, but I aren't been looking." Lester headed toward the firepit and Ben set down his crosscut saw – no Mac-Guigan had ever figured it worth the expense to get hooked up to the nearest power line a mile away, and Ben didn't figure it worth firing up the generator to run a skill-saw – and lifted a fresh plank onto the sawhorses to measure his next cut.

Lester came back from the firepit saying, "I guess not, unless I dropped it in the fire," and laughed. "Or unless it's in my tackle box, like Jake's socks," and laughed some more. "Say, I was kinda surprised to see you still here. I thought after your wife come up last night, you'd maybe gone home with her?"

Ben didn't consider him and Lester Perkins to be well-enough acquainted to ask each other those kinds of questions. But, in lieu of being rude, he just said, "Nope."

"Well, see ya."

"Yup."

Ben started lining up his next cut, then stopped. As far as he could remember, Lester Perkins didn't smoke.

Funny, too, now that Ben thought about it, that Jake Mac-Guigan had said he wasn't all that well-acquainted with Lester Perkins, either. Apparently it was only a few weeks ago that Lester had started gassing up at MacGuigans' garage instead of the Irving closer to home. Ben didn't put in enough shifts at the garage to be sure who was a regular and who wasn't, but Lester had always been as chatty as though he was one. Shaky Jake had ribbed Ben once about Lester having a crush on 'the big fella,' because Lester had asked more than once, *"Oh, Ben not working today?"* And it had only taken Jake's offhanded mention that he was thinking of doing some brushcutting and burning for Lester to volunteer himself and his young fella to lend a hand.

After what Bonnie'd told him last night, Ben could suspect

a particular reason that added up with all those odd little things about Lester Perkins. But then, that implied a lot of forethought on Lester's part, to be keeping close tabs on Ben for so long ahead of a handy time to borrow the truck and butcher the trees. And it didn't make sense for Lester to've kept on leeching around, like a dog at the edge of the pack, so long after the fact. Maybe hang around a little, so he didn't suspiciously suddenly stop coming around anymore, but Lester had been hanging around a lot.

Since Shaky Jake had started camping out at his hunting camp, there'd been any number of guys dropping by for a beer, other MacGuigans and their friends. Any one of them might've noticed Ben's truck sitting there, and remembered seeing those big maple trees at the back of the Marsdens' woodlot.

Ben left the next plank waiting on the sawhorses and tramped down to retrieve his truck key from its so-clever hiding place under the mud-mat. Although the damage to the trees had already been done, he was a bit nervous about anybody rolling around Membertou County in his very recognizable truck, especially since he now had a criminal record and would be presumed guilty until proven innocent, if he could prove it.

Then again, whoever'd borrowed his truck already – if anybody actually had – might've thought to get the key copied. So he started up the truck and ran it just long enough to put a felt pen dot on the gas gauge glass, at the tip of where the needle stood. Then he put the key back under the mat and went back up to his flooring factory.

He still couldn't puzzle out any fathomable sense in why, if Lester had been the one who'd done the truck and the trees, Lester would keep on leeching around. Even making up zip-headed Zippo excuses to drop by. Well, that sort of thing – puzzling out why someone might've done this or that – was more along Bonnie's line, and she wasn't around to lend a mind. That set Ben's mind and heart back onto the treadmill he'd kept getting funnelled onto for the last two months. Maybe he could sidetrack himself by wrenching out some old floorboards with a crowbar and hammering some new ones in.

On the next day that Ben was needed to do a shift at the gas station, he was putting seven dollars into a crusty old lady's new car when his VFD pager went off. Shaky Jake came running out of the service bay with his own pager in his hand, trailed by the nephew who was learning auto mechanics the old-fashioned way. Jake shouted, "Leave 'er go, Ben, the young fella'll finish 'er off!"

Ben let the gas gun trigger spring shut, left the nozzle in the old lady's filler hole and ran for Jake's truck. Since the firehall was only a few corners away from the garage, and Jake took the corners on two wheels, Ben and Shaky Jake were the first there and into their gear, and took off first in the pumper truck. Which was just as well, since the fire was reported to be somewhere back in the woods on Priory Village Road, and nobody had more than a vague idea of where that road was. Nobody except Ben, who'd done a fair bit of exploring of back roads in his younger days. An old fella had told him there used to be some sort of little monastery back there, till they gave up fighting the blackflies.

Even after twenty years of taking VFD calls, the kick-up of adrenalin in Ben made the pumper truck's speed and siren and flashing lights seem secondary. He slowed the truck down, though, as he got near where he half-remembered the mouth of Priory Village Road was. He wasn't expecting any signage for it, so wasn't disappointed. He'd also expected the road to be overgrown and filled with potholes, but it wasn't as overgrown as he'd expected. There'd been a fair bit of traffic up and down that road lately, and wider wheelbases than ATVs. Ben bore down on keeping up as much speed as possible without leaving him no reaction time to deke around the bigger potholes. Not that there was much room to deke.

Shaky Jake's "Holy fuck!" made Ben raise his eyes from where they were trained on pothole watch. A pickup truck was barrelling down the narrow road head-on towards them. Jake shouted, "Swerve!"

"Where the fuck to? *He'll* swerve." And the pickup truck did, braking and skidding off the road into the ditch weeds. "Damn fool, playing chicken with a firetruck."

"That was Lester."

"Huh?"

"Lester Perkins. I got a good look at him as we went by."

"Well, we'll prob'ly get a closer look at him on the way back – prob'ly have to tow him out."

A gust of wind threw a cloud of thick black smoke across the road. Ben slowed down drastically. When the cloud cleared, he didn't speed up again, because the cloud had turned into a column of smoke off to his right, and there was a truck-wide trail through the woods leading off in that direction. It turned out to be a short trail, through just a narrow fringe of woods. Beyond it was a clearing with a piece of machinery in the centre, which was glowing and sparking and giving off more black smoke than Ben would've thought possible for its size. All around it were piles of cordwood and lumber, and other pieces of machinery with lots of jerry cans of gas to feed them.

The chief was in the next truck behind Ben and Jake's, and got everybody humping to get the machine drenched in foam before it blew. When that was done and there was no more black smoke, and the piece of machinery was just a big marshmallow sundae glob of dripping foam, Ben leaned back against the side of the pumper truck, breathing slowly to slow down his heart. The beers back at the firehall were definitely going to taste good.

Shaky Jake MacGuigan, propping himself up with one hand on the truck beside Ben, said, "Did you see what it was?"

Ben said, "Oh yeah." Ben figured Shaky Jake and the rest of the crew had seen what it was, too, before it got smothered in foam. It was the machine that drove the Jaws-of-Life, rigged up as a wood-splitter. Ben started to laugh.

Jake said, "What's funny?"

"Oh, I just realized what Bonnie meant by 'an even funnier possibility.'"

"Huh?"

"When I told her about the special oil that machine needs – so the damn fools that stole it would either have to identify themselves to the factory, or fake it with plain oil and have it seize up

– she said, 'There's an even funnier possibility.'"

"Yeah?"

"What she meant was, they might keep on running it dry after the fancy oil ran out, it'd overheat and start a fire and – who they gonna call?"

Jake said with him, "The Volunteer Fire Department!"

"Wait'll I tell Bonnie!" Ben could hear her laugh already. "Wait'll I . . ." He realized he wouldn't be doing that, and trailed off. "Oh, hell." He moved away, stuck his hands in his pockets and ambled around the clearing as though curious about what-all was there.

Good old Lester had definitely had some ambitious operation going. Besides the wood-splitter, he had a portable sawmill, and besides the hundred-or-so cords of firewood, he had stacks and stacks of rough lumber. Probably most of it had been taken off Crown land, but one stack of wide planks set apart from the others looked suspiciously like bird's-eye maple. Once the Mounties had done documenting the evidence, Ben would have to have a talk with them about the return of stolen property.

* * *

Bonnie got a phone call from Darcy. After a bit of general chat about how things were going at either end of the line, Darcy said, "Dad called."

"Oh?"

"He asked me did I still keep in touch with any of the furniture makers I knew when I was working for Donald Fisher. I told him, sure – once you get enough sawdust up your nose it's in your blood. Dad got the bird's-eye maple back from the police, and wondered if the guys I know would like to buy it, and I said no doubt. I mean, it's too late to save the trees."

"That's true." That came out as just conversational "um-hm," the kind of sound you make to assure the other person you're paying attention. The subject of the conversation seemed farther removed from Bonnie than a phone line to the city.

"Dad said to send the cheques to you and it'll pay the mortgage for a while."

"Oh. Thanks, dear." Well, it *was* their mortgage, still, and had been their trees.

"*I* didn't do anything. I'm just doing what Dad asked me." There was a pause, as though Darcy was expecting Bonnie to say something more to that. When Bonnie didn't, Darcy dropped it and went on to, "Mom, this is kind of silly, but it's been bugging me. You remember when we were eavesdropping on Dad and the other guys around the fire talking about hockey players, and Dad said that thing that they seemed to take as a natural fact, but he never said a name? I don't get it."

Bonnie clucked, "Kids today. I was never much of a hockey fan, but even *I* knew that. Maurice 'The Rocket' Richard. Never was another one like him, and . . ." Bonnie was intending to finish her sentence with the same faraway tone, but something closer to home caught in her throat. ". . . and never will be again. I, uh, have to hang up now."

* * *

Ben sat alone, sipping watered-down Membertou County Springwater, and staring into the flickering fireplace at the MacGuigans' hunting camp. Jake MacGuigan had patched things up with his wife and moved back home, but Ben didn't mind not having to make conversation. The dancing flames – red, yellow, blue and all kinds of combinations – painted pictures from the last thirty years: sweat-soaked Bonnie with a red, new baby; Moyle with his high school football uniform so covered with mud you couldn't read the number; Bonnie's stone-set face maintaining that she'd done the world a favour by putting Charlie Warner in jail . . .

In between the pictures, Ben's wandering and drifting periodically tripped over a question that couldn't possibly matter a damn to anybody, but nonetheless kept pestering him. Why the hell had Lester Perkins kept nosing around, after he'd already snuck Ben's truck to steal the wood?

11

On a misty morning, Bonnie walked Melissa down to the schoolbus, both carrying armfuls of pussy willows. The kitten paw buds brushing against Bonnie's cheeks were even softer than the air of what the old folks called "a soft day." Once Melissa and the pussy willows were safely aboard the bus, Bonnie walked back home, feeling the gravel of the road shoulder squelch beneath her feet. The ground was still too wet for digging. She guessed she had maybe another month before she'd have to decide whether she should call Ben's friend who brought his little tractor up to till their vegetable garden every year, or whether she should leave it to Ben, or whether there might not be a "their" vegetable garden.

When Bonnie got home, the antique cuckoo clock in the kitchen – "antique" only in the sense that it was older than she was; Sears wasn't renowned for its Olde Worlde handcraftsmanship – told her she had time for another cup of coffee before loading up her cleaning gear. Loading and unloading didn't take much back and forthing, now that she didn't have to worry about things freezing in the car overnight. The radio news came on with: *"There was a tragic event in Butcher's Corners last night . . ."*

Well, there were tragic events in Butcher's Corners most nights. Rose Coffin was about the only person Bonnie knew of who'd been born there and got out into another kind of life.

Bonnie was about to tune out the story as just run-of-the-mill depressing, but it turned out to be anything but run-of-the-mill, even for Butcher's Corners. Two young men and a young woman shot to death in a mobile home. Bonnie could picture the kind of ramshackle mobile home that would be on the outskirts of Butcher's Corners, but she couldn't picture what would make somebody kill three people who hadn't been on earth long enough to make murderous enemies. The radio explained it to her: the two young men were best friends, one had stolen the other's girlfriend, the betrayed one had shown up drunked-up at the rented trailer where the love of his life and the friend of his life were shacked-up, shot the two of them – several times, in a frenzy – and then shot himself.

Bonnie muttered, "What a sin," about the fact of life that wasn't taught to young people, and maybe couldn't be. The fact was that the situation that seems impossible to live with today can seem possible tomorrow, just with the shifts and twists of time. What made it even worse in this case was that the young man who'd stolen the other's girlfriend was out on bail, awaiting trial for operating a growhouse. The radio announcer didn't extrapolate from that, but to Bonnie it meant that probably the third party in the triangle would've soon been removed from the equation anyway. Maybe for no more than a couple of years, but two years is a very long time when you're only twenty years old.

The last names of the three dead kids – Macleod, O'Neill, Porter – were so common around Membertou County that Bonnie didn't guess she had any connection to any of them. Their pictures in the next day's newspapers, probably from their high school yearbooks, didn't call up any recognition.

But Bonnie found out she did have a slight connection, as more information came out around coffee shops and kitchen tables. Young Sam Macleod, the one who'd done the shooting, was the son of Shauna Macleod, whom Bonnie had nattered with many times across the counter at Wade's Groceteria & Take-out & Video. Shauna had always been uncannily unfailingly cheerful, regardless of ugly weather or surly customers. Rumour had it that

Shauna was so cheerful at work because it was the only time she could get away from her home and husband. Bonnie didn't count or discount rumours about people she didn't know very well. One thing that wasn't rumour was that the shooting had been done with a handgun, not a rifle or shotgun that most country homes had on hand.

The next time Bonnie was in Wade's – to get 3-for-3-bucks-for-3-days old videos to get Melissa through the weekend – Shauna seemed just as chipper and cheerful as always. Maybe the crows' feet behind the vintage batwing glasses were a little deeper, or maybe that was just the light. Bonnie said across the counter, not loud enough to draw other customers' attention, "I was so sorry to hear about . . ."

Shauna just tightened her mouth and nodded, then tapped her finger on *Finding Nemo* and said, "That's a good one." It made Bonnie wonder whether Shauna's constant cheerfulness was uncanny or canny. But then, what would Shauna Macleod have to hide about something that was already all over the news? Probably just her emotions.

Melissa was happily watching *Finding Nemo* for the third or fourth time, and Bonnie was in the kitchen rolling her week's supply of cigarettes, when the phone rang. Bonnie picked it up before Melissa could get jolted out of her blessed quietude.

"Mrs. Marsden, it's Corporal Kowalchuck. I've been given some information I think you and your husband should be made aware of."

"Ben isn't here. Isn't *living* here. At the moment."

"Oh. I'm sorry to hear that. I thought that situation would've been resolved." Bonnie could almost hear him catching himself saying too much about someone else's personal business. "But, um . . ."

"There's no phone where he is, but I could get a message passed on to him to call me, if it's important."

"Oh, it probably won't affect either of you at all, just thought you should know – *I* should've been informed weeks ago, but only found out by accident. It concerns Jack Burton."

Bonnie's back jerked stiff, as though the phone had just shoved a needle in her eardrum. Jack Burton was supposed to be long ago and far away, for good. She said, "What about him?"

"Well, you remember I said it seemed strange that Mr. Burton didn't appeal his conviction?"

"Yeah."

"Well, it seems that for some lawyerly reason I'm not privy to, it was decided to wait until he'd been in Kingston Penitentiary for awhile, and his very expensive Nova Scotia lawyer got partnered-up with a very expensive Ontario lawyer. Then they filed an appeal, on various grounds, including a possible violation of Mr. Burton's Charter Rights. So he's out on bail pending the outcome."

"He's *out?*"

Corporal Kowalchuck seemed to've expected that kind of reaction. "Not as much as that sounds. The reason I called was so you wouldn't hear just half the story somewhere, and think you and Ben had reason to worry. One of Mr. Burton's bail conditions is that he can't leave the city of Kingston without police permission. And he has to report to a parole officer twice a week."

"That'd still give him three or four days to take off and come back without telling anybody. He could easily –"

"*And*, unknown to Mr. Burton, he is under police surveillance on the days he doesn't have to report. Now that the Superintendent's Office finally thought to inform me of the situation, I've contacted the Kingston Police Department, and they've agreed to contact me immediately if Jack Burton should drop out of sight. So until and unless you hear different from me, there's nothing for you to worry about."

As poker-faced and -voiced as Corporal Kowalchuck was, Bonnie had had enough conversations with him to know that normally he would've proceeded directly from what he'd finished saying to *Bye for now,* without a second's pause. After about three seconds, Bonnie said, "There's something you're not telling me."

"Well, um, now that the case is being appealed, the Crown is collecting and reviewing all the evidence filed from the original trial. They discovered that . . . It seems that the pen, the toy that you recorded Mr. Burton's confession on —"

"It's disappeared?" Bonnie remembered Jack Burton's chisel-hard voice telling her he knew that Membertou County RCMP hadn't requisitioned a wire, *"Don't ask me how."*

"No, no, not at all. It's perfectly intact, and in the original envelope it was filed in. But . . . it's been wiped."

"What?"

"Erased."

"What?"

"Oh, it doesn't necessarily mean anything nefarious. Remember that the Air India trial fell apart because some genius officer went and erased all the wiretap tapes. And that was a *mass* murder. As my grandmother used to say," Corporal Kowalchuck slipped into an exaggerated accent that Bonnie assumed was Ukrainian, "'Fewer harms get done by skullduggery than skullnummery.'"

"Well, anyway, the Crown still has the certified copy, the CD dub they played at the trial."

"Well, um, actually, since it was made for the purposes of the original trial, after the trial was over, and no appeal filed, that disk was recycled and reused."

Bonnie reheard the Corporal's voice saying, *"the . . . trial fell apart . . ."* She said, "So me and Ben are It."

"How's that?"

"Tag, you're It."

"Ah. Actually, you might very well not even be called upon to testify. The appeal might well not even make it past the preliminary hearing. As I said, I called to make sure you had a picture of the actual situation, instead of being alarmed by half-pictures. The actual situation is that Jack Burton is still safely in prison, just that the prison is now the city of Kingston, instead of just Kingston Penitentiary."

"Yeah. Okay."

"Bye now."

Ben wasn't working the gas station that day, so Bonnie just

left a message for him to call her. When he did, and she told him what Corporal Kowalchuck had told her, he muttered, "Sonuvabitch. They can keep that poor dumb kid's bullshit video on file, but they lose a flat-out murder confession. You all right?"

"Yeah." The question was a bit annoying, as though he thought the little woman was scared and needed him to protect her. "I just called because Corporal Kowalchuck asked me to pass on the information."

"Well, lemme know if you hear anything more. Okay?"

"Sure. Bye now."

After she hung up, Bonnie sat staring out the kitchen window at the pink-gold spring sunset light on the trees fading to black. Telling Ben what Corporal Kowalchuck had told her, going over it again, brought up something that prickled at her. Insurance. Back when Jack Burton had first been charged, Corporal Kowalchuck had guessed that one reason he'd decided to forego bail was insurance. Insurance against getting blamed for any 'accidents' that happened outside while he was inside, because the police knew he did his own dirty work. He had the same kind of insurance now, at least for anything that happened outside the city limits of Kingston, Ontario.

Bonnie wondered if maybe Jack Burton's high-priced lawyers might've been able to argue away the ruling that sequestered him there – Charter Rights and all – if he'd let them. And she wondered just what 'under surveillance' meant during the three or four days between his meetings with the parole officer. The Kingston police couldn't very well just call him in for questioning whenever they felt like it; lawyers in Hersh Greene's league would slap them with Police Harassment so fast and hard their heads would still be spinning. So, 'under surveillance' probably meant a glance through the front window of a restaurant he was known to hang out in, or across a crowded tavern. A glance at a medium-sized man with grey hair and beard and glasses. For that matter, how well did the parole officer, or rotation of parole officers, know the man who reported to them as Jack Burton?

Bonnie went into Robbie's old room and dug out one of the

cardboard boxes stacked in the closet, the one felt-penned MAPS. In his pre-driver's-licence days, Robbie'd had a thing about collecting road maps, from anyone From Away who came to visit, and from Moyle's wanderings. Bonnie spread the map of southern Ontario on the kitchen table, and found Kingston and the Toronto airport. About two-and-a-half hours apart. And this was an old map. Bonnie remembered hearing there'd been a toll highway built through there, where people could drive even faster than on a regular freeway. So, someone who could afford to fly full-price Business Class could easily get from Kingston to the Halifax airport in four or five hours. An hour's drive from there, or even less, could put them anywhere in Membertou County.

For that matter, there was bound to be some kind of airport at Kingston for commuter airbusses and private planes. Jack Burton could certainly afford to charter a small plane now and then, and there were a number of cropduster-type airports dotted around rural Nova Scotia. But no, those little airports had to keep fairly accurate records. The only records of who came and went through an international airport were passenger lists, thousands of names every day.

Bonnie lit another cigarette – the other one had burned away in the ashtray while she was looking at the map, so it really didn't count as two in a row. Something pinged at the back of her mind. She'd only been thinking of herself, and Ben by extension, in relation to what Jack Burton might or might not be up to. But there was someone else, something else, too much coincidence, maybe.

Bonnie went down the basement and dug through the box of old newspapers and not-so-old ones. She wasn't all that hopeful; at this time of year, when they only ran the wood furnace at night, they went through a lot of newspapers and kindling. But it turned out there was one section left that had an article on the murder/suicide in Butcher's Corners, the article with the pictures of the three dead kids when they were alive.

Bonnie smoothed out the wrinkled article on the kitchen table and read it through again. As she'd half-remembered, Howard

Porter – the one who'd taken up with, and taken off with, his best friend's girlfriend – had been out on bail awaiting trial for operating a hydroponic marijuana growhouse. One certain thing about Jack Burton was that one of his business activities was setting up and financing growhouses. Just ask Billy Vickers.

What if, maybe, what Jack Burton was up to was mopping up? What if he had enough money socked away to retire, get out while the getting's good, but didn't want to spend the rest of his life waiting for the tap on the shoulder? He'd have to take care of a few loose ends. Loose ends like the growhouse kid who might lead to other charges pending if he beat the charges for murdering the other growhouse kid. Loose ends like the two people who were the only remaining evidence for *"I flambéd the little bastard."*

But when Bonnie read back through the details of the murder/suicide – as much detail as got into the newspapers – she couldn't see how it could've been anything but what it seemed. Howard Porter and Carol O'Neill had been curled up on the couch watching TV, when Samuel Macleod burst in on them in a drunken rage, with an unregistered, automatic pistol he'd got from somewhere-or-other. Samuel Macleod fired all the bullets in his clip, except one, into the two lovers and the couch they were curled up on. Then he put the pistol to his head and fired the last bullet. Like most crimes, there was nothing complicated or masterminded about it. Just sad and stupid.

It wasn't until Bonnie was giving Clyde his flashlight walk around the yard before bringing him in for the night that she realized what was wrong about the story in the newspaper. If Samuel Macleod was in such a drunken, jealous rage, blazing away with a Saturday Night Special he'd bought in the backroom of some pool hall, how was it that he calculated precisely how many bullets he pumped into his ex-friend and ex-girlfriend? Counted down exactly to the last bullet?

On Monday, Bonnie only had a couple hours' work in the morning. On the way home, she dropped by Wade's to drop off the videos – a good excuse to see if Shauna Macleod happened to be working that day. There was a young woman at the cash register counter, and no customers roaming the aisles. Bonnie was turning to go back out the door, when she caught the glint of Shauna's steel-wool hair ducking down behind the meat counter.

Bonnie headed over. Shauna Macleod was rearranging trays of chops and sausages in the display cooler. "Hi, Shauna."

"Oh, hi there, Bonnie," came out as perkily as always. "What can I get for you today?"

"Actually, um, I'm not shopping for anything," which wasn't entirely true. "I just wondered if maybe you felt like stepping out for a smoke break."

"I don't have any cigarettes."

"I do."

The red-brown eyes behind the batwing spectacles glanced around warily. Bonnie suspected that Shauna'd got the glasses when they were fashionable, around 1962, and since then had always found other things to spend money on than herself. "Well, I wouldn't say no to a smoke."

There were a couple of picnic tables outside the takeout door, and the windbreak of the building made for passable sitting weather. Bonnie gave Shauna Macleod a cigarette and a light, and lit one for herself. Shauna sucked in her first drag like someone who'd been wanting a cigarette for a long time. Bonnie said, "I don't mean to be nosy, Shauna, and it's none of my business – well, maybe it is, in a way, I'm not sure. But I think maybe what happened in Butcher's Corners, with your son and all, didn't happen at all like the police and the newspapers say it did."

"*Do* you?" That burst out so fervently that Bonnie felt like she'd just loosened the cap on a bottle about to burst. Gushing out came, "Oh, I *know* Sammy would never – he might hurt himself, but never anyone else – he's not like his father. Oh, I don't mean his father would – no, of course I don't mean *that*, but . . . Sammy didn't even *like* guns, wouldn't go hunting. When I told the police that, they just looked at me like I was just being a mother."

Shauna Macleod took a dainty handkerchief out of her sleeve

and dabbed at her nose and eyes, then went on, "Of course Sammy felt awful bad about Carol dumping him for Howie. Who wouldn't? But the way Sammy was trying to get over it was stay away from them, stay away from anyplace they might come around. And when he went out that night, he was in good spirits, said, 'Leave a candle in the window, Ma,' then stopped himself in a jokey kind of way and said, 'No, that would be a fire hazard, leave a battery-operated, safety-certified lighting device.' Well, that was Sammy, always joking, even if sometimes the words were so twisty you didn't know what the joke was."

"Did he say where he was going?"

"No, and I didn't ask. You know, after they hit a certain age, you don't want to pry, make yourself a nuisance."

"Yeah, I know what you mean." Bonnie's eyes went to Shauna Macleod's cigarette as she tried to take another drag. Shauna's fingers had hourglass-crimped it so tight nothing would come out. Bonnie took the plastic cigarette case out of her purse and took out another cigarette, saying, "Here, sorry, sometimes I'm not as careful with the rolling machine as I should be, and you end up with an empty gap in the middle."

"Thanks. Anyway, all I know for sure – besides knowing for sure Sammy didn't do what they said he did – is he got a phone call that night, and as soon as he hung up he went for his coat."

"Do you know who called him?"

Shauna Macleod shook her steel-wool-capped head. "It was an older man – I mean older'n Sammy and his friends. All he said was, 'Sam there?' and then I called Sammy to the phone. So, I couldn't say for sure if it was a voice I'd ever heard before or not."

"Was it a . . ." There was that prickly feeling again, crawling up Bonnie's spine. ". . . *dry* voice?"

"Yeah, that's a good word for it. Dry like a desert."

Like windblown sand, sifted through Bonnie's mind.

"Why?" Shauna Macleod said eagerly. "Sounds like someone you know?"

"Maybe. I'm not sure. So, um, Sammy didn't say who it

was?"

"No. But I did hear one funny thing – I mean funny strange, not funny funny. Though with Sammy sometimes one could be the other. You don't want to be an eavesdropping mother, so I was just going about my kitchen business and not listening in on what he was saying to the phone. But he laughed just before he said this one thing, and that caught my ear. What he said was, 'Better'n a pre-frontal lobotomy.' Any idea what that means?"

"No," Bonnie said truthfully. "No idea. Well, I know what a pre-frontal lobotomy means, vaguely, but I don't have the vaguest idea what Sammy could've meant by what he said." But there was a tiny pinging from the sonar in the depths of Bonnie's memory. "Well, thanks for telling me what you could, Shauna, and I'm sorry to've bothered you –"

"No bother at all. Thank you for caring. No one else does. I'd give anything to have my Sammy not remembered as a murderer and a suicide."

"Well, um, I'll let you know if I find out anything. But, believe me, I'm not that good a person, I've got my own selfish reasons."

The road home from Wade's wasn't long or complicated and Bonnie'd driven it a thousand times, but nonetheless she made an effort to push away what she'd just heard, to keep from getting sucked in and blanking out and going off the road. Once she was safely back in her kitchen, with a pot of tea on, she took the reins off her sound-memory. Out of all the things Shauna Macleod had said, what kept coming back was, *"Better'n a pre-frontal lobotomy." "Better'n a pre-frontal lobotomy . . ."* After a number of replays on her in-skull stereo system, Bonnie started to hear it in a voice that wasn't Shauna Macleod's, or what she imagined Samuel Macleod's might've sounded like. It was a deeper, rough-worn, gravelly voice – not sandy like Jack Burton's, and without that terrifying, straight-razor, cold-chisel edge lurking under the surface. There was a melody behind it, a bluesy melody, but the voice didn't have the murderousness of Howlin' Wolf and that gang. And the words weren't exactly *"Better'n a pre-frontal lobotomy . . ."*

Bing! *"I'd rather have a free bottle in front of me than a pre-frontal lobotomy."* It was a lyric from an old Tom Waits song. Just the kind of music Jack Burton was likely to have on his car stereo, and to play in the background while he was making arrangements with the patsies who operated his growhouses. No doubt the young stooges thought they were very cool and in with Jack The Man, when they tossed off in-jokes to him about the music he'd turned them on to.

Now Bonnie could see what had happened that night in Butcher's Corners, after Jack Burton had called Sam Macleod and said something like, *"Don't say anything about this to anybody. I managed to slip away for a bit — a short bit — and I figure my best bet to get a handle on what's been going down, is have a few words and a few drinks with you. You got more smarts than all the rest of them put together. So, I got a bottle of rum in the trunk with your name on it . . ."*

Night Scene. Exterior of a peeling-sidinged mobile home on the edge of Butcher's Corners. A generic-looking car pulls up. Jack Burton climbs briskly out of the driver's door, wearing driver's gloves, and out of the passenger door stumbles and fumbles . . .

Bonnie had to think back to the high school yearbook photos in the newspaper, to get a picture of the passenger. Samuel Macleod was chunky-featured, dark haired. Maybe now that he'd been out of high school for a couple of years, he'd grown a goatee, like so many young men these days . . .

Sam rubber-joints, and flops back against the car to keep from falling. Jack Burton takes a pistol out of his pocket and says, "You just stand right there, Sammy, till I come around and get you."

Sam slurs loudly, "Sure, Jack, whatever you —"

Jack Burton hisses, "Keep it down! Don't want to give the surprise away." He shakes his head at stumbly Sammy and clucks, "Kids today. A few pulls off a free rum bottle and you can hardly stand up." He points Sam toward the trailer and gives him a push. "Just walk straight up to the doorstep — as straight as you can — and knock on the door. I'll be right behind you."

Sam starts unsteadily walking, but murmurs over his shoulder, "What if they won't let me in?"

"Don't worry — once they open the door a crack I'll push you in."

"But —"

"Sammy, didn't your mother ever tell you it's not polite to ask questions of people who've got loaded pistols against your back? You just do what they tell you. Once I'm inside you can take off back out the door and keep on going — this is between me and Howie."

Bonnie's imagination shifted her to what was going on inside the mobile home, while Jack Burton and Sam Macleod were walking towards it. The newspapers said that Howard Porter and Carol O'Neill were curled up on the couch watching TV when Samuel Macleod burst in and shot them, and then shot himself. So, the couch would have to be on a straight line from the front door. Probably an open area, with a kitchenette to one side of the doorway and a sort of living room on the other. And probably a new, big-screen TV and an old, ratty couch. From the high school yearbook pictures, Carol O'Neill was blondish, with a snub nose and freckles. Howard Porter was thin and dark-eyed.

The young couple on the couch aren't paying as much attention to the TV as to each other. After all, they may well soon be separated for a long time. Or maybe they won't be, if Howie can work a deal with the police, but that's just maybe. A knocking at the door makes them sit up and take their hands off each other.

Howard Porter stands up and takes a step toward the door, as Carol O'Neill murmurs, "Who'd be coming around at this time of night?"

Howie, seeing through the front door's window, says, "It's Sam."

"Oh, hell. Don't let him in."

Howie, moving toward the door, says, "I'll just go see what he wants . . ."

"You know what he wants. But he can't have it anymore."

Howie unlocks the door and opens it a crack. Before he can say anything through the crack, the door flies open as Sam Macleod seems to burst in — actually pushed by Jack Burton. Carol jumps up to help

Howie, yelling at Sam to get the hell out. Then both young lovers see Jack Burton, and the gun, and they go very silent.

Jack Burton says pleasantly, "Hello, Howie. Hi, Carol. Been a while."

Howie says nervously, "Jack, I . . . You know I wouldn't –" then cuts himself off.

"Wouldn't what, Howie? You two lovebirds just sit back down on the couch where you were cuddling, and we'll have ourselves a little conversation."

As Howie and Carol do what they're told, Sam reminds Jack Burton, "You said I could go, once –"

"Oh, you're going all right, Sammy." While he's saying that, Jack Burton grabs Sam's arm to hold him, claps the pistol to Sam's head and pulls the trigger. Carol screams. Jack Burton puts a bullet each into Carol and Howie, and they're dead before Sam hits the floor. Jack Burton empties the rest of the clip into the corpses on the couch, intentionally missing once or twice, to give the impression of someone firing wildly and furiously. Then he crouches down beside Sam Macleod and puts the gun in the dead, right hand, saying, "Consider this your gun now, Sammy. No, really – I want you to have it . . ."

Bonnie snapped out of it there, and back into her kitchen. She was missing something, some other step Jack Burton would've taken to cover his tracks. Just putting the gun in Sam's hand wouldn't do it, because . . . She remembered from old movies and murder mysteries that firing a handgun left gunpowder stains on the shooter's hand. Maybe modern gunpowder burned much cleaner, but then, modern crime labs and forensics were much more sophisticated. So, when Jack Burton fired bullets into the two already-dead kids on the couch, he was coldly counting-off to make sure there was one bullet left in the clip. It didn't make sense for a drunken, frenzied kid, who didn't even like guns, to be that methodical, but it made perfect sense for Jack Burton. So, then . . .

Jack Burton wraps Sam's dead fingers around the gun, fitting the forefinger through the trigger guard. With his gloved hands wrapped around Sam's hand and the gun, Jack Burton points it in the general direction of the couch and squeezes Sam's finger to fire the last bullet. "Nice shootin', Sammy." Then Jack Burton lets Sam's hand fall back to the floor, stands up and looks around the room, nodding, and says to no one but the audience in his head, "Well, my work here is done." He calmly walks back out to his car, knowing that people around Butcher's Corners don't stick their heads out their doors at the sound of gunfire, at least not till long after the shooting stops.

Bonnie nodded to herself. That scenario made more sense than the murder-suicide almost nobody'd questioned – at least as far as sense could be applied to a twisted creature like Jack Burton. She remembered she had a cup of tea in front of her, and picked it up. It had gone cold, but not as cold as she had. If those three young people had died the way she imagined, all Jack Burton would've had to do when he left Butcher's Corners would be to stop somewhere to get himself cleaned up on his way to the airport, and in a few hours he'd be sitting innocently in Kingston, planning how to finish mopping up the last of his loose ends: Bonnie and Ben Marsden.

But, if what happened that night had happened like she imagined, or something like, there was still no way to get anybody else to believe it. Jack Burton had left no evidence, nothing to contradict the neatly tied-up package he'd left for the police and the coroner. There was nothing concrete she could use to convince the police that Jack Burton had murdered Sam Macleod, Carol O'Neill and Howie Porter, and next on his list were a couple of middle-aged yokels who'd gone and stuck their noses in his business.

Then something clicked about something she been'd thinking just a minute ago. She'd thought that all Jack Burton would have to do when he left Butcher's Corners was stop somewhere to get himself cleaned up on his way to the airport. Why had she guessed he'd have to get himself cleaned-up? He wasn't exactly someone who liked to present an elegant appearance. And from what she believed had happened in that trailer, there hadn't been much of a tussle, and shooting people wouldn't get him bloodied-up. Except . . . Right. When he put the pistol to

Sam Macleod's head and pulled the trigger, there must've been a fair spout of blood over Jack Burton's hand. Maybe he'd even had to burn whatever jacket he was wearing, if the blood spattered as far as his sleeve. Which meant that there should've been blood on Sam Macleod's hand and sleeve, if he'd shot himself. There wouldn't be, if someone else had shot him.

Bonnie reached for the phone.

12

Bonnie was pleasantly surprised that Corporal Kowalchuck was actually in the office to take her call, and even more so when he said, "Funny thing, I was meaning to call *you*."

"Oh?"

"To set your mind at ease. After our last phone call, on the subject of Jack Burton, you set me wondering whether the Jack Burton that the Kingston police have under surveillance may not always be the actual Jack Burton. Not that I mean any lack of confidence in another police force, of course."

"Of course." She didn't say, *Hell, if your* own *damn force can't keep evidence from being erased, why should you trust anybody else's?*

"I asked them for some information, and a favour, and they complied. Apparently, they usually have coffee in styrofoam cups. In Mr. Burton's last meeting with his parole officer, a few days ago, the parole officer complained that some damn fool had forgot to fill out a requisition form, and served Mr. Burton his interview coffee in a ceramic cup instead. After the interview, the cup was dusted for fingerprints, and they match perfectly with Jack Burton's fingerprints on file."

"Oh."

"Apparently Mr. Burton seemed rather amused by it all. At the end of the interview, he very carefully pressed the ball of his thumb and his fingertips against the sides of his cup."

Bonnie was willing to bet that Jack Burton found few things more hilarious than police officers' clever tricks. She said, "Well, thanks for checking it out. But, like I said before, that still leaves him three or four days in between times he has to report to the parole officer. You can't sneak fingerprints off him when he's out on the street – or what *seems* to be him is out on the street."

A small hint of a sigh came through the phone line. Bonnie could almost see Corporal Kowalchuck in his office, looking at the stacks of paperwork on other cases he had to deal with. She decided she'd better get straight to it. "Corporal, those three young people who were shot to death in Butcher's Corners a couple of weeks ago . . . ?"

"The murder-suicide, yes."

"What if it wasn't a murder-suicide, but a triple murder?"

"Um . . . How's that?"

"Those kids had been involved in a growhouse, hadn't they?"

"Howard Porter was awaiting trial for a hydroponic marijuana operation. We had no direct evidence against Samuel Macleod or Carol O'Neill, but we had our suspicions."

"One of Jack Burton's businesses was financing growhouses. What if those three were planning to inform on him to keep themselves out of jail, or one of them was, or he thought they were? What if he saw the perfect opportunity, the perfect cover – the classic love triangle, with three screwed-up kids?" Bonnie could hear herself starting to sound too imaginative, too many what-ifs. She bulled on. "If he shot Sam Macleod first, and then the other two right after, you wouldn't be able to tell, would you? That the other two weren't shot first."

"Um, no, not if it was only a few minutes. But, there were powder burns on the side of Samuel Macleod's head, and powder residue on his hand. So, he definitely pressed the gun to his head and pulled the trigger."

"But was there blood on his hand and arm? I mean, if he pressed the gun to his own head and pulled the trigger, there'd be blood spattered on his hand, wouldn't there?"

"I wouldn't say *spattered*." He sounded like he was getting hesitant about discussing this kind of gory detail with a civilian. "There is actually a surprisingly small amount of blood inside the brain, and the brain cavity. And whatever, um, spattering might've happened, would be from the exit wound."

"Oh." That set her back. But after a quick rethink of mental pictures that made her a little queasy: "But there'd be at least a bit of blood thrown from the entry wound" – she wasn't sure if that was the right term, but it seemed to go with 'exit wound' – "when the bullet went through the skin and all. So there'd be at least a few drops of blood on his hand, wouldn't there?"

"Yes, there would be, and I'm sure there *were*."

"Are you *sure*? There's a thing magicians call 'Misdirect,' and they wouldn't have a name for it if it didn't work. Every other detail of the crime scene pointed in one obvious direction. With such an obvious cut-and-dried murder-suicide, who'd think to notice that one little thing?"

"I didn't notice. But then it wasn't my case. All I did was secure the area for the Major Crimes unit. I'm sure they investigated thoroughly."

"I'm sure they did, but . . . It wasn't like that was the only case they had to investigate that week, and they didn't have any reason to suspect it was anything but what it seemed to be. Maybe nobody'd think to imagine about that little detail, unless they had as much reason to be as nervous as me."

"Well, I guess I could request the photos of the scene be shipped back from Halifax, and see if I can see – if that'd make you feel safer. I don't know when I'll be able to get to it."

"When you can." Although she wanted to scream, *Now! You're a public servant and I'm the public.* "Thanks."

"Well, you're the only reason Jack Burton was in jail, I guess you've got a right to be nervous about him being out of jail. Bye now."

After Bonnie hung up the phone, she sat wondering. Maybe she was being a hysterical, lonely woman, letting her imagination run wild because her real life was such a mess. Maybe she was right, and her life and Ben's were in serious danger – maybe even Melissa's, if she got in the way – all because Bonnie Marsden couldn't resist sticking her stubby little nose where it didn't belong.

One thing was certain: if she just sat there wondering, she was going to frazzle herself in circles. She needed something to do. The car was still speckled with winter crud that rain couldn't wash off, hardly a good advertisement for a cleaning lady, and it was a sunny enough day to get out the hose and the scrub brush.

* * *

After Corporal Kowalchuck hung up the phone, he sat drumming his fingers on the stack of paperwork he should be dealing with, but thinking about Bonnie Marsden. The woman was definitely, truly scared – who wouldn't be? He pushed the paperwork aside and picked up the phone, to ask Kingston to check a certain date against the dates Jack Burton had to check in with his parole officer. The night of the Butcher's Corners killings had been two days after Jack Burton's previous appointment, and two days before the next. After Kowalchuck got off the line to Kingston, he keyed-up his e-mail address book to find the listing for evidence file storage in Halifax.

A few afternoons later, Kowalchuck was easing his patrol car along the tail end of a winding, gravel road through the woods. He saw a few vehicles parked up ahead, and muttered a few un-Mountiely words. He'd been hoping for only one vehicle. Oh well, couldn't be helped. He parked behind the last vehicle, and decided to leave his uniform cap off, but his ordnance belt on. As he climbed the wide path through the woods, he began to hear voices, in the comfortable tone that human voices took on in the open air.

What he saw when he came out of the woods was something like four hooky-playing schoolboys having a weenie roast.

Except that the schoolboys were Big Ben Marsden, Shaky Jake MacGuigan, and two others closer to Ben's size than Jake's, both with the dark brows and bulgy shoulders of most MacGuigans. All four heads turned to look at Kowalchuck coming out of the woods, and the looks weren't friendly. One of the dark MacGuigans said loudly, without deigning to rise from his lawn chair, "You got no right to come on our property without a warrant. Clear off."

Kowalchuck stopped a few steps away from them and said, "This isn't official. I just wanted to have a few words with Mr. Marsden."

All three MacGuigans looked protectively at Ben. Ben said, "Jeez, Corporal, when I said I wanted to tell you about what these boys got up to in Truro last week, I meant in private."

There was a fast-frozen silence, then an explosion of laughter, as hot dog ends and buns were hurled at Ben with shouts of, "Rat! Stool pigeon! Fink!"

Ben stood up and said, "I'll walk you back to your car, Corporal. You can have your words on the way."

Once they were in the woods and walking slowly, Kowalchuck said, "Did your wife pass on the information about Jack Burton?"

"I got the message, yeah."

"The Kingston police assure me that he's never left their jurisdiction, but . . ."

"But you're not so sure."

"Well . . ." One thing Kowalchuck definitely wasn't sure of was how to proceed with the conversation. Squirrels were yelling, *"Trespasser"* from the trees. He said, "I don't have enough manpower to put a watch on your home, and I can't request outside assistance on a hunch. Budget restraints are –"

"*Budget restraints?*" They'd been walking down the path side-by-side, but now Ben stopped and turned to face him, so Kowalchuck did the same. "We're talking about a goddamn maniac coming after my wife and you're talking about *budgets?*"

"I don't *know* that Jack Burton has ever violated his parole.

He has made no verbal threats — has he?"

"Well, he wouldn't, would he? Fella'd have to be an idiot to tell people he's gonna kill 'em."

"So I have no hard evidence of any impending situation." That sounded pathetically bureaucratic, even as it was coming out of his mouth. "I'm only the Detachment Commander of a three-constable hole-in-the-wall in the backwoods of Nova Scotia. I can make sure that the constable on night patrol passes by your house whenever he can, but . . ."

"But otherwise me and Bonnie are on our own."

"I'm only a phone call away. At any given moment the duty constables might be occupied at the other end of the county, but I've instructed the dispatcher to inform me immediately of any 911 call from your number, even when I'm off-duty."

"What's your response time?"

"If I'm at home asleep, from my place to yours, maybe twenty-five minutes."

Ben Marsden's response to that was a black laugh. Kowalchuck didn't need to have it pointed out how much could happen in twenty-five minutes. Or five minutes. Ben said, "Yeah. Looks like I'll be sleeping back at home the next little while." Which was exactly what Kowalchuck wanted to hear. But then, Ben added, "If it's okay with Bonnie."

"Why wouldn't it be? Oh, I guess that's none of my business."

"Nope. Nothing personal, Corporal, but it's just something between me and Bonnie. Anyway, looks like she and me're gonna have to live with each other until Jack Burton's back in jail."

"There's a message you can pass on to Bonnie for me, if you would. She'll know what it means."

"What's that?"

"Well . . ." Now that he was about to say it, Kowalchuck's sense of testimony made him hedge. "I suppose it could've just been the angle of the photographs, or the light, but, as far as I could see, there was no blood on Samuel Macleod's hand."

* * *

Bonnie was setting things on the counter, getting ready to make supper. Melissa said, "Is it still Kraft Dinner if we're having it for supper?"

"Well, if we put sausage in it it's Kraft Supper."

"Oh." As Bonnie cut some real cheese to add in, she wondered whether Melissa was old enough to comprehend or care that a lot of people in the city, and other parts of the country, called supper 'dinner,' and dinner 'lunch.' Before Bonnie could decide, Melissa said, "There's somebody in the driveway."

Bonnie looked over at Melissa, standing with her head cocked, listening. Bonnie couldn't hear anything but the hum of the ancient fridge, but Melissa's ears were a lot younger. Bonnie felt a kick of fear, after dwelling so long on the night Jack Burton's car pulled into the driveway of that old trailer. It was still daylight, though, so Bonnie just said, relatively calmly, "I don't think so, honey. Clyde'd be barking his head off if –"

"It's Daddy!" Melissa ran to one of the back windows. Bonnie saw through it the old red truck with the black door.

Bonnie said tightly, "He's probably just going to get something from the barn."

"No, he's coming in!" Melissa charged down the stairs to the back door, as Ben stepped through it, and hurled herself into his arms.

Bonnie muttered, "If you're going to leave us alone, leave us alone." Then she said aloud, and crisply, "What do you want, Ben?"

Ben paused near the top of the steps, with one arm cradling Melissa and the other hand on the bannister. He said, "Your friend Corporal Kowalchuck dropped by, asked me to pass on a message to you. The message is: There was no blood on Sam Macleod's hand."

"Oh God." Bonnie had to clutch the edge of the counter to steady herself. It was one thing to imagine it, and another to know it was true. And to know that the monster under the bed was real. She'd never in her life wished so much that she hadn't been right. "Melissa, go downstairs and watch TV for awhile. I'll hold up supper."

"But –"

"I'll still be here, pumpkin," Ben said as he set her down. "Scoot along now."

When Melissa was gone, Ben said, "What's that mean – no blood on Sam Macleod's hand?"

"It means the murder-suicide in Butcher's Corners wasn't a murder-suicide. It was set up to look that way, by a very clever and nasty person."

"Yeah, that's sorta what I figured it meant." Ben moved further into the kitchen and reached up into the space between the top of the kitchen cupboards and the ceiling. That was where he kept the keys to the gunbox, because no one else could reach. "Mind if I sit down?"

"Huh? No, go ahead. I think there's still some tea left in the pot." She half-filled two cups with the dregs, and sat down across the table from him. It was very strange, having him back in their home but still so distant. But then, the whole world was very strange just now.

Ben said, "Come dark, I'll take out the twelve-gauge and load it up. I only keep birdshot on hand, but Jake MacGuigan had a half-a-box of buckshot shells lying around. You remember how to work the pump action? Just in case, you know, something happens when you can get to it faster'n me."

Bonnie knew he was also saying, *Or in case I can't get to it at all, because he's already got me.* She said, "Yeah, just pump it back and forth and pull the trigger." Very early in their marriage, Ben had taken her out duck-hunting once. Once had been enough. If men's idea of a good time was sitting in a swamp freezing their asses off, they were welcome to it.

Ben travelled his eyes around the kitchen, saying, "I don't like having a loaded gun around the house, but . . ."

"Put it up on top of the fridge. I'll make Melissa promise not to go near it."

"Not go near the fridge?"

Bonnie started to laugh, then stopped herself. Just because he was back in the house didn't mean things were back like they were. She said stiffly, "How many nights do you plan on coming back?"

"As many as it takes. Till we know for sure Jack Burton's back in jail. Days when I ain't got work on, I'll catch up on my sleep on the living room couch."

Bonnie resisted saying, *Oh, got it all decided, have you?* She said, "It's going to be damned confusing for Melissa. She's been confused enough the last two months."

"Well, I'm sorry, but I can't help that. You made your choice –"

"*I'm* not the one that walked out!"

"I mean you made the choice to call the Mounties on an innocent man."

"Charlie Warner wasn't innocent."

"That's the way you see it. Seems like you and me have come to see a lot of things different. But there's only one way to see the situation we're in now."

"'We' isn't just you and me. If Jack Burton *is* going around tying up loose ends – Melissa'd be here, too."

"Yeah, that crossed my mind."

Bonnie decided not to take that as a sarcastic *Well, duh*. She told herself to push her resentments aside for now, and take on faith that he was doing the same. She said, "Maybe tomorrow I should call Muriel and get her to take Melissa overnight for the next little while. I'd have to come up with some sort of story for Melissa."

"Well, uh, that could be a good idea, except . . . Something occurred to me while I was driving over, see what you think. As things are now, Melissa's always with us, or on the schoolbus, or at school. If she's staying with somebody else, and Jack Burton can't see a way to get rid of you and me unsuspiciously . . . Wouldn't be the first time a witness's child got kidnapped till the trial was over."

Bonnie felt a saw blade twisting in her guts. Her first impulse was to say, *He wouldn't*, but of course he would. She let out an

170

agonized, "Oh, no."

"No?"

"I meant oh, no, you're right. This is *crazy* – we've got laws and police and a whole system to protect us, and here we are, loading up a shotgun to protect ourselves."

"The police and the laws are real good at cleaning up messes after they happen. Anyway, maybe we're getting ourselves all worked up for no good reason. Maybe what happened at Butcher's Corners happened just like the papers said it did, and the no blood on the hand was just a fluke. Wouldn't that be funny?"

"Hilarious."

Ben didn't actually bring the shotgun out until after supper, when the light outside started turning those pretty sunset colours. Bonnie slung Melissa a line about a skunk that'd been hanging around at night, and would eventually either spray furry Clyde, or kill the baby chickens due to arrive soon.

Clyde usually didn't want to stay inside for long after he'd been brought in for his supper, but tonight wanted to stick around and enjoy the pack being all back together. His bladder wouldn't hold all night, though, so while Bonnie was giving Melissa her bath, Ben put Clyde back out on his line till his usual bedtime. Melissa wanted her father to tuck her in, and Bonnie surprised herself by not minding. Sitting alone in the kitchen, Bonnie could hear their voices, first Ben's soft-edged rumble, "See you in the morning, pumpkin."

"Promise?"

"I promise."

When Ben came back into the kitchen, he took the shotgun down off the fridge and set it on the table, then sat down beside it. He said, "I, uh, wanna turn the lights off in here – don't want him to be able to see me and the shotgun. If there's any him to see. No use both of us sitting here in the dark."

Bonnie said, "You'll be all right?" then felt foolish for saying it.

"Oh, yeah – plenty of coffee in the pot, and I'll leave the radio on just loud enough to keep me company. I'll lie down when the sun comes up. Here," he took the VFD pager off his belt, "I'll turn the volume off so you don't get woke up if there's a fire call, but you know where the emergency button is?"

"Yeah."

"I'll bring Clyde in after he's had a while to remember what he's supposed to do out there."

Bonnie stood up with the pager in her hand, and then didn't quite know what to do, whether she should kiss Ben good night, or keep up the distance he hadn't really reached across yet. She settled for stopping as she stepped past him, and putting her hand on his shoulder. He put his hand on top of hers, looked up at her and nodded, "We'll be all right."

* * *

After Bonnie had gone downstairs, Ben got up and turned off all the upstairs lights. He stood a moment looking out the windows over the kitchen sink, wondering whether he should turn on the yard light – just a double flood lamp fixture mounted on the back of the house. With the yard light on, he'd be able to see everything that was going on between the house and the treed slope down to the trout pond. But no, with the yard light on, anyone moving around out there would know they could be seen from the house, and would creep along under cover of the blackberry rows, or the big pine tree, and all the other shadow-casting things out there. With the yard light off, and the light of even a half moon being brighter than the kitchen darkness his eyes were adjusting to, he'd be able to see more than someone out there might think.

He couldn't see much but vague shapes inside the kitchen, but he'd navigated his way around that kitchen in darkness a thousand times before. And the LED lights – blue numbers on the microwave, red dots for the phone and the radio – gave him navigational points he hadn't had on nights when the power went out. More than a few winter nights he'd sat up alone till morning, because somebody had to babysit the wood furnace, make sure it had just enough of a fire to keep the house barely liveable, but not so much that it overheated itself with no electricity to run the air blower.

Ben poured a tiny bit of local flavour into his coffee, and sat wondering what possible scheme Jack Burton might have hatched to murder him and Bonnie, without it looking like a murder. Maybe a firebomb – people dying in housefires wasn't uncommon. But no, Ben had been in the VFD long enough to know there weren't many ways to hide traces of arson from modern police forensics, and the few ways that might work required a lot of careful, inside prep. And if the police forensics didn't get you, there were the insurance investigators –

A sudden burst of crazy sound made Ben's hand jump to the twelve-gauge. Then he laughed at himself, and took his hand off the gun before he did himself a damage. It was a crazy sound, all right, downright cuckoo – Bonnie's grandmother's cuckoo clock, that'd been hanging on the kitchen wall since the old girl went into the nursing home. He must've heard it only about a hundred thousand times before.

Ben went back to trying to think of what Jack Burton might be thinking of as a way dead Marsdens wouldn't lead straight back to him. Maybe make it look like a botched home invasion – there'd been a double murder in Membertou County disguised as a botched home invasion only last year, and it was only Bonnie's curiosity that kept the police from buying the disguise. But no, Jack Burton wouldn't have much time after the gunshots to make the house look home-invasion ransacked, not if he wanted to get away clean. This wasn't Butcher's Corners, where neighbours didn't get too curious about gunshots in the night.

Or maybe Jack Burton didn't give a shit if the Marsden murders looked like plain old murders, since he'd be plainly a thousand miles away in Ontario when they happened. But no, the only person on earth with enough motive to murder Ben and Bonnie Marsden was Jack Burton. If the police started seriously digging into airline records and such, maybe they'd come up with something. It wasn't Jack Burton's style to leave dead bodies lying around with no possible explanation but him.

Or maybe Jack Burton was still in Kingston, Ontario, had never left since he got out of jail there, and had no intentions of leaving until his appeal came through.

The radio played an incredibly stupid commercial. The female DJ came on after with a surprisingly raunchy joke about it, so it was getting to be that time of night when she figured she could get away with it. Pretty soon, Ben figured, he should get up and go bring Clyde in. Pretty soon . . .

"Ben!"

"Daddy!"

The voices were coming from a long way away, and hissing like whispered shouts. Small hands were pulling on his arms. A pack of dogs was barking and baying and roaring and growling. No, it wasn't a pack, just Clyde outside, rupturing his throat trying to bark and growl at the same time. And the voices and hands were Bonnie and Melissa.

Ben jerked awake and jerked his head up off his chest. Bonnie hissed, "There's something out there. Or some*one*. I'm going to call 911."

"Um, no, don't." Ben gave his head a shake, as much to clear out the sand as to underline no. "Jesus, Bonnie, if we go calling the Mounties every time Clyde starts barking at something in the dark . . ."

"This is different."

"Maybe, maybe not. Remember the boy who cried wolf." He pushed off from the table to get to his feet, and shuffled over to the window above the sink. "Damn, can't see him. If he's running back and forth, he's doing it all in the shadows."

Bonnie said, "I'll turn on the yard light."

Ben said, "No" and noticed that he seemed to be saying no to everything she said. "The second the yard light comes on he'll sit down and look at the house and we won't see what direction he was barking in. Probably just a fox, or a skunk, or the neighbours' cat. For that matter, he might just be barking 'cause he's not used to being left out this long at night. My own damn fault.

He might keep it up all night if I don't go bring him in."

It was Bonnie's turn to say, "No!" but more sharply than any of the times he'd said it.

"Look, think about it, Bonnie. Uh, Melissa, cover your ears a minute, pumpkin." He waited a second, then, "They covered?" No reply. He whispered just loud enough to cross the arm's length between him and Bonnie. "Think about it. If *he* was out there, what'd he be doing just standing around while the dog barks at him? And if he *was* out there, what's he gonna do – shoot me when I go out to get the dog? He'd know you're in here, and you'd hit 911 the second you heard a gunshot. It don't make sense. Okay?"

"Yeah, okay," but she didn't sound happy about it.

Ben raised his voice a couple of notches, "Okay, pumpkin, you can take your hands off now. If it *is* Mr. Skunk, or Mr. Porcupine, let's hope I get to Clyde before they get too well-acquainted. Like I said, leave the yard light, I'll take the flashlight."

"And the shotgun," came from Bonnie.

"I only got two hands." He used them to start feeling his way to the stairwell down to the back door. "Stumbling around in the dark, trying to juggle it and the flashlight and Clyde's leash, I'd probably blow my own head off. Or Clyde's. It'll be safe where it is, long as you keep Melissa away from that end of the kitchen table." He felt for the little nook in the wall beside the back door, and the flashlight was there as it should be. Clyde's leash was hanging beside it. Ben turned the doorknob and gave it a tug. It didn't want to move. He'd forgotten he'd locked the door, not something they usually did. He remedied that, and stepped outside.

Outside, Clyde's snarling and roaring sounded even louder. Lucky it was Clyde. If old Floyd had ever got that frantic on the line, he would've broken the cable by now, or chewed through it, or broken his teeth trying. As Ben walked toward the sound, he searched the flashlight beam around for Clyde. When it found him, Clyde didn't sit down and turn toward the light, as he would've with the yard light. Ben flicked the flashlight beam in the direction Clyde's nose and noise were pointed. Nothing nearby but a barely budding lilac bush. Whatever Clyde was barking at – stray dog, cat, skunk, fox, porcupine – was likely lowdown to the ground, and wouldn't show unless the flashlight caught its eyes.

Ben crouched beside Clyde, who sat down and stopped barking, but would still need a bit of calming down before his shaking and shifting slowed enough to safely hook the leash on and the line off. "What's the big to-do, buddy? Yeah, it's all right, I'll have you in in a minute."

From out of the darkness came that voice like dead leaves scuttering across a drumhead. "Hello, Ben."

13

Ben's spine went cold. He started to stand up and turn toward the voice, but – "*Don't* shine that light in my direction – point it at the woods. I'm out of the dog's range, but you're in mine."

Ben didn't have to be told what that meant, or told twice to angle the light away. But he continued with the turn he'd started, till he was pointed toward the voice. Now he could see a vague, man-sized shape beside the lilac bush, with the last of the moonlight painting the grey hair dull silver.

There came that dry, little cough that might be a laugh, then, "Yeah, I figured if the dog went on long and loud enough you'd come out to look around. Come talk to me." Ben slowly stepped forward. "And point the light toward the house, now. No, not straight on, more of an angle. That's better. The flashlight's a nice touch – makes it even harder to see there's two of us."

Ben said, surprised that his throat hadn't gone entirely too tight to say anything, "The police told us you're still a thousand miles away."

"I got a little brother looks a bit like me. Not a lot, but put him in a grey wig and glasses, grizzle-up his beard . . . I show up in person for my dates with the parole officer, then hop on a plane and make little visits home. Lotta people wouldn't believe it, but I clean up pretty good in a business suit. You should see my Air Mile points. Except they're all in phony names. Hell of a waste."

"Little visits like to Butcher's Corners a couple weeks ago."

That brought a couple of little cough-laughs. "Yeah, I figured your nosy little wifey might suss that out. Kind of hoped she would. But the police don't buy it, do they?"

"She's got 'em wondering."

"Yeah, but not wondering very hard."

Ben could see the gun now, or the glint of it, pointed dead centre. He knew he was too big a target, and couldn't move fast enough, to knock it aside long enough to get a punch in. One good punch would be all he needed, but he could see he wasn't going to get it. Unless Jack Burton got distracted, or too complacent. Smart-crazy was still crazy, and maybe if the crazy part could get sidetracked enough for the smart part to stop paying strict attention, even for a couple of seconds . . . Ben said, as conversationally as he could manage, "Why, uh, why the hell would you hope Bonnie'd suss out Sam Macleod didn't shoot himself?"

"To bring you home. I wanted to have a conversation with the two of you together, and as soon as possible after you moved back home. This worked out perfect. I happened to be in the neighbourhood, on other business, when I heard you'd quit playing campfire girl. So here I am, on your first night home. Timing couldn't be better. You see, I've had an eye on you for some time, though the eye didn't know who was paying it."

"Huh." Ben nodded at the answer to a question he'd asked himself. "Lester Perkins."

"Yeah, I could've killed him when he —" Jack Burton interrupted himself with a laugh, "but I didn't — when he got greedy, working his own stupid, little scam, and just about blew the whole deal. So, I got my employee department to hire on somebody more discreet."

Ben wondered who. One of the MacGuigans? Whoever it was wouldn't've known who they were working for, maybe even thought they were working for Bonnie. Anyway, it didn't matter now.

"Let's go see what the inside of your house looks like, Ben."

"I don't think so."

"What?" There was a tiny flash of moonlight on eyeglass lenses, as Jack Burton cocked his head sideways. "This isn't a cap-gun, Ben, and I don't think you're bulletproof."

"You're not going to shoot me out here. You're a lot of things, but you're not stupid." *Please don't prove me wrong.* "You know Bonnie's in there. One gunshot and she'll hit 911. She's got my fire department pager, too. That's a lot of sirens and witnesses right quick. So, you're not going to shoot me out here."

"I'm not planning on shooting anybody. I told you I wanted to have a conversation with the two of you together. The gun's just the way to get me in the door."

"Oh?" Ben tried to not sound too sceptical. His knees were starting to ache from standing stiffly, and his mid-section from being clenched while the gun was pointed at it. He very much wanted to sit down and have a drink.

"I had a lot of time to sit and ponder on ways you and me and Bonnie could get out of our current situation – I mean, besides the obvious. I came up with a couple of possibilities."

Bens's eyes had grown accustomed enough to the dark and the constant focus on Jack Burton that he could make out the general shape of the face above the beard: the snub nose, the wire glasses-rims around the pale eyes. Not well enough to read expressions, but they probably weren't readable anyway. Ben said, "What are they? I mean, the couple of possibilities you came up with."

"I said I wanted to talk to the two of you together."

"What about?"

"*Damn*, you're stubborn." Jack Burton's free hand flailed in the air, but his gun hand never wavered. "All right, just basic. First possibility is, you give up doing odd jobs for farmers and start doing 'em for me. I got a three-year plan toward early retirement – *cushy* early retirement. Same'd go for you. You'd see more money in three years than you have in thirty. Money buys freedom, Ben. Live free or die. I spent the first thirty years of my life shovelling shit, and eating it. I'm gonna spend the last thirty eating caviar in Margaritaville."

Ben wondered if Jack Burton could possibly be crazy enough to truly believe Ben would throw in with him. Then again, given that the life Ben had been living for the last thirty years seemed to've hit a dead end, maybe it didn't sound all that crazy. Either way, it seemed that the diplomatic thing to do under the present circumstances would be to let the man with the gun carry on saying what he had to say. Which was: "All my tribulations came from greed, hiring on cheap labour. I thought even a dimwit, weedhead kid would have enough brains to realize it's better to spend a year of your life behind bars than lose the whole rest of it. I thought wrong. But *you* – you're a stand-up guy, you've been around . . . and you think like me."

That came at Ben so weird that he blurted undiplomatically, "No, I don't!"

"You don't, eh?" There were a couple of little cough-laughs, then, "And just what would've happened if what your wifey played back to you on that James Bond pen hadn't sounded like enough to nail me with? I would've ended up just like Billy Vickers. Except in my case, the constabulary wouldn't've dug hard for forensics. 'Tsk tsk, too bad – too bad we don't know who to pin the medal on.'"

Ben wasn't sure what would be safe to reply to that. His left hand, pointing the flashlight away from them, was starting to shake, maybe from holding the same position so long. He very slowly moved his right arm across his body, to change hands. Jack Burton's vaguely visible, grey-and-white head nodded, to show he knew what Ben was doing and it was okay. It was an awkward position, holding the flashlight pointing left with his right arm slanted like a Boy Scout Mountie belt. But once he'd done the shift, Ben realized he'd accidentally put himself in a better position to sweep the gun aside for long enough to get a punch in. His left fist wasn't as certain as his right, but all he needed to do was stun him. But even a slim-chance opportunity depended on Jack Burton's attention going unrivetted for a second or two, and that hadn't happened yet.

Ben said, "What's the second possibility?"

"The same kind of job offer Bonnie got from the Wild Rose Credit Union, except with another company Bert Jackson deals with out there, and a queen-size signing bonus the company wouldn't know about. If you two wouldn't feel comfortable about getting subpoenaed for my appeal, and having to perjure yourselves about early onset Alzheimer's, I could arrange for new identities. Sort of my own, private, witness-relocation program. Everything's going privatized these days."

Ben didn't know what he should say. He had no doubt Bonnie wouldn't go for it, but maybe she could string Jack Burton along enough for him to go away happy, and then a quick 911 would have the airport Mounties screening every outgoing passenger. But surely Jack Burton knew that people tended to tell a man with a gun whatever he wanted to hear?

Ben wished to hell Bonnie was there, with her faster and wider way of sniffing out all the complexities. He was quite sure he was missing something, some little detail in what Jack Burton had said and done, that Bonnie would've twigged to. But Ben still couldn't see any possible way Jack Burton could shoot them without getting suspicion all over him. So Ben said, "Okay, we'll go inside and talk to Bonnie."

"*Finally*. We'll take the scenic route, outside the circuit of the dog. Keep the flashlight pointed in front of you, I'll be right behind you, and it won't be a flashlight I'll be pointing. You cast a giant shadow, Ben."

Ben walked slowly to the near edge of the vegetable garden, and along its border. The dog lines, whether old Floyd's or Clyde's, had always been set to keep them from messing with the garden. It crossed Ben's mind that the garden would need him to get hold of buddy with the tractor soon, if there wasn't too much rain. Or if *he* wasn't planted before then. He told his so-called mind to stop wandering and bear down on what might be on Jack Burton's mind.

Jack Burton said conversationally, "Yeah, it was probably an insult to say you think like me . . ."

Ben couldn't think of anything safe to reply to that, so he just kept ambling along at a slow march, and the gun didn't prod his back to walk faster.

". . . but you know the same thing as me. You know the bullshit fantasy is bullshit. The fantasy that lets nice people do worse things than me." A couple of cough-laughs added punctuation, along with the slow swish of their shoes through dewy grass that'd be due for mowing soon. "I am *not* a nice person, but I don't torture, and I don't whack people who aren't gonna whack me. You need a higher principle to do those sorta things, and I got no principles. And *you* – you know the bullshit without even having to smell it. You know it in your bones."

"Uh, what do I know?"

"That we ain't the Crown of Creation. *Clown* of Creation, more like. Semi-educated monkeys at best. That dog of yours is no more different from you and me than an ATV from an SUV."

"Well, in some circumstances, an ATV's a lot superior to an SUV."

The cough-laugh this time burst out so explosively that Ben almost turned around to see if Jack Burton had hemorrhaged his sinuses. "Hah! Told you you knew." That burst-out cough-laugh obviously hadn't burst Jack Burton's sinuses, but it seemed to've cleared them, because Ben heard a deep, nostril-inhalation behind him, then, "That garden smells almost good to go."

"Yeah." Ben knew what Jack Burton was smelling: the thawed, bare earth just beginning to turn from mud to garden soil. What Ben couldn't quite smell, though he was trying his damnedest, was exactly what plan Jack Burton had brought with him tonight. All Ben had been able to pick up were a few contradictory whiffs.

"You use weed-killer and that?"

"Nah, haven't been any chemicals used on this property in fifteen, twenty years."

"Good, that's good. Organic's more work, but worth it in the long run. That's how I plan on doing my garden in Margaritaville. Ain't much better fertilizer than seaweed off the beach. Hey, whadda you figure the Oilers' chances in the playoffs?"

"I, uh, aren't paid much attention to the NHL since the Habs told Guy Lafleur to get with the new program or go home."

"Hah! You're right – trying to turn a jet fighter pilot into a bus driver. I saw him in an exhibition game here, with the Nordiques, and he was playing like he used to. It was his thirty-ninth birthday and he scored a goal."

Clyde, who'd settled down to low growls while Ben and Jack Burton were standing talking, had started barking increasingly louder the farther they moved away. Now he'd worked himself up to full-out roaring and bellowing. Jack Burton growled, "Doesn't your damned dog ever shut up?"

Ben called out, as loud as he could without blatantly shouting, "Floyd, quiet down! It's all right, Floyd! Take it easy, Floyd!"

* * *

Bonnie was hunkered over the sink, peering through the window above it. All she'd been able to see out there was the flashlight beam, locked in one spot for a long time, but now moving more or less toward the house, though not straight toward the back door. Maybe when the flashlight had been in that one spot so long, it was because Clyde had got himself tangled up in something, and it had taken Ben awhile to get him untangled and calmed down, and to scare off whatever Clyde had been barking at. Maybe the slow, circle-route toward the house was to give Clyde a chance to remember his bladder before going inside. Now Bonnie could maybe see Ben's shadowy bulk behind the beam, or maybe she was just imagining it.

All she'd been able to hear all that time was Clyde. But now she heard what Ben was calling out. Melissa obviously heard it, too, because she whispered, "Why is he calling Clyde Floyd? Floyd's dead."

And, Bonnie extended that without saying it aloud, *Floyd died fighting off an intruder in our home.*

Bonnie gripped the curl of the counter and pushed against it to straighten her spine. Breathing was suddenly something she had to do consciously, trying to keep it slow and even against the rabid thumping in her chest. She said, in as calm and clear a voice as she could manage, "Go over to the yard light switch please, honey, but don't turn it on until I tell you. Just put your hand on it." She saw the vague shape of Melissa moving across the kitchen, and heard her hand brushing its way up the wall. She knew the switch was a bit of a reach for Melissa, but not a full stretch. "You got your hand on it?"

The small, tight voice came out of the dark, "Yes, Mommy."

"Good. Now, keep your hand on it and close your eyes and keep them closed. When I yell 'now,' you flick the switch. Can you do that for me, Melissa?"

"Yes, Mommy."

"Good girl."

Bonnie measured the three steps to the kitchen table, and carefully felt her way along the shotgun lying on it. Once she had her left hand wrapped around the pump-stock and barrel – just barely around, given the size of her hands – and her right hand around the curve of the stock behind the trigger guard, she stepped back to the sink counter. She held the shotgun up perpendicular in front of her, and very gingerly angled it forward and down. When she felt and heard the muzzle touch the window glass, she angled the shotgun back perpendicular again, and worked the pump slide down and up to cock it. The metallic clicks seemed to echo like cymbal clashes in the cold quiet of the kitchen. "Quiet as the grave," her grandmother would say.

Through the window, Bonnie could see that the flashlight beam had got a lot closer, probably nearing the top of the garden. Pretty soon it would probably turn and start moving along the back of the house toward the back door, crossing in front of her window. She waited.

* * *

When Ben reached the top border of the garden, he turned left onto the scavenged-flagstone path that ran along behind the house. The soft sound of his slow-march footfalls through the grass turned hard: thud . . . thud . . . *thud* – it hit him, what Jack Burton was up to, what the plan was. It was right there in what he'd said at the beginning, that he'd wanted to 'have a conversation' with Ben and Bonnie as soon as possible after Ben moved back home. And *"here I am, on your first night home. Timing couldn't be better."*

Everything Jack Burton had said and done since then now added up perfectly: the 'two possibilities' that not even a maniac could believe Ben and Bonnie would go for; the flat-out confession to the Butcher's Corners killings, with perfect trust Ben would never repeat it to anybody; even the offhanded sidetracks into hockey and organic fertilizer. It was *all* organic fertilizer. The point of it all was just to keep talking, to keep Ben distracted and thinking in other directions, until they got inside the house. And then, as soon as they'd stepped safely across the threshold . . .

Ben had seen and heard the standard story a hundred times before, on the news, in newspapers, around coffee counters: long-suffering wife finally kicks husband out; husband vows to change behaviour, but she won't buy it; estranged husband builds up frustration and possessiveness, barges back into his old home and shoots wife and then himself, plus whatever children happen to be home. *"Tsk tsk, who'd ever've thought it of the Marsdens?"* "Well, he did *drink, you know. Done jail-time, too." "Just goes to show you never know what's going on behind closed doors, even next door."*

Ben's slow-march grew even slower, then stopped. He felt the muzzle of the gun prodding his back, and heard Jack Burton saying, "I didn't tell you to stop walking."

"Maybe you don't think you did, but you did. Another murder-suicide, eh? Different scenario, but just as typical."

Jack Burton yanked Ben's arm to turn him sideways, facing the house, and kissed the mouth of the gun to Ben's temple. The steel circle was colder than the night air. "I could do it right here right this second, Ben, if you don't start moving. How would they know you didn't do Bonnie inside and then come back out to do yourself, taking one last look at your house?"

"You shouldn't've said that, Jack. Now I got no doubts at all."

"You stupid son of a bitch, do you *want* to die?"

"No, I surely don't, but . . ." A thousand things passed through Ben's mind. Things like that he'd already fathered three good kids who could take care of themselves, and Melissa well on her way; that the dam which turned the swamp into a trout pond had already lasted just dandy through a hurricane and a couple of nasty winters, so would no doubt keep on standing without him around to patch and tend it; that he and Bonnie had already had a lot of good years together. They were things Jack Burton wouldn't understand if Ben had a hundred years to try and explain them to him. But there was one very immediate thing that Jack Burton definitely would understand, but didn't know about. Jack Burton didn't know that Bonnie had a shotgun sitting on the kitchen table. If she heard a gunshot outside, and then Jack Burton came through the door without Ben to hide behind – twelve-gauge buckshot at close range should do just fine. "Nope, I surely do not want to die. But this is as far as I go."

* * *

Bonnie had watched the flashlight moving along the flagstone path behind the house, but then it had stopped, a little short of being directly straight-line in front of her window, and stayed where it stopped. Her arms were starting to shake from holding the shotgun up in front of her. Much longer and she'd drop it. A bit of an angle would have to do. She asked herself, *Are you really going to try this insane thing?* then shouted, "Now!"

Bonnie smashed the shotgun barrel down through the glass, as the butt swung up to meet her shoulder. In the sudden glare of the yard lights, she saw two men standing close together, Ben on the right and Jack Burton on the left. Jack Burton was wheeling around to gape toward the crash and the light. Bonnie pointed the gun at him and pulled the trigger. The explosion in the kitchen almost burst her eardrums, and the kick-back almost knocked her off her feet, but only almost. She jerked the pump-slide back and forth and fired again, then again, then again . . . Then there was nothing coming out of the shotgun but clicks, the kitchen was thick with smoke, and Melissa was screaming. Probably she'd been screaming since the first gunshot, and Bonnie hadn't been able to hear her.

Bonnie said breathlessly, "It's all right, honey, it's over," or at least she dearly prayed it was. With all the thick, grey, acid-tasting smoke in the kitchen, she couldn't see what was outside, even with the yard light on. And all she could hear from outside was Clyde barking and baying even louder than before, or maybe he just sounded louder with the window broken open.

Bonnie laid the shotgun down on the counter and slumped into the nearest chair. Her right shoulder felt like somebody'd been working it over with a meat hammer. She said, "You can turn the light off now, honey, and open your eyes, and come over here."

Melissa's screams had settled down to whimpers. The light on the smoke through the broken glass went out. An instant later, Clyde's rabid roaring suddenly stopped. Bonnie heard Melissa feeling her way along the table edge, and reached out. Melissa climbed up onto her lap, and Bonnie put her arms around her.

The back door opened, and Clyde came bounding up the stairs, flinging himself around Bonnie and Melissa's chair, licking every piece of skin he could get his tongue on. Behind him, much more slowly, came a figure blurred by smoke and darkness, but unmistakably Big Ben Marsden.

Ben paused at the top of the stairs, leaning on the bannister. Bonnie said, "Is he . . . ?"

"Oh yeah. Two or three times, I'd say."

Bonnie could hear the grunt as he pushed himself off from the stair rail and started into the kitchen. He stumbled, and Bonnie heard a pain-stab intake of breath. She said in terror, "Ben?"

"No, I'm fine. Just . . . did my knees a bit when I dove out of the way. I'm gettin' too old for this sorta thing."

The red pin-light on the phone cradle disappeared and was replaced by the pale yellow light coming out of the keys. Bonnie heard three key beeps, and then the yellow light moved up to cast an eerie glow on a patch of Ben's cheek and the corner of his right eye. After a few seconds, Ben said into the phone, "My name's Ben Marsden, Pisiquid Village. This is a Mountie situation, for the Raddallton Rural Division. You'll want to make sure it gets to the Detachment Commander, Corporal Kowalchuck. Message is 'problem solved.' You got that? . . . Well, your Caller ID should be telling you that, but you can tell him I'm . . . at *home*. . . . No, I won't stay on the line, but if you wanna stay in your job, you better get that message through right quick. Sorry to be rude, but I got a dead man in my backyard and I'm tired."

There was a beep, and then some fumbling sounds, and the yellow glow was replaced by the red pin-light. Bonnie could hear, and vaguely see, Ben semi-blind-walk to the table and along it. Instead of lowering himself into the nearest chair, as she'd expected, he kept going till he was right up next to her. Then he grunted his way down to sitting on the floor beside her chair, and lolled his head against her arm. She raised that arm from around Melissa, and draped it across his neck and shoulder, so his head was against her side. His hand came up and laced its fingers through her other hand, the one on the arm around Melissa. Melissa's little hand settled on top of the two of them. Bonnie could feel Clyde curling up on the floor, between and pressed against her foot and Ben's knee.

After about a minute, Bonnie could tell by their breathing that both dog and daughter had sunk safely and securely into sleep. Well, not exactly sleep. Bonnie had seen it happen before, to creatures of all shapes and sizes. After some horrible, frightening and exhausting event that you don't understand, all you want to do is curl up in a cocoon and go away for awhile.

Bonnie understood what had happened that night, more or less, but she didn't understand what it meant for her and Ben. At least not in any way she could explain to herself. The differences that had made him walk out, and her not compromise herself to bring him back, would still be there in the morning. But so would he. Some things just couldn't be talked out and resolved, no matter what the TV therapists said. They became things you didn't talk about, but kept in mind. They just became part of the ongoing story – ongoing she hoped. Her and his opposite opinions about the law and right and wrong and all those important things hadn't changed. But all those important things had just been trumped.

About the Author

Alfred Silver was born in Brandon, Manitoba, and grew up in various places across the Canadian prairies. His secondary education ranged from day-labourer to short-order cook to nude modelling to playing in bar bands, with a few eccentric electives along the way. He now lives with his wife in a farmhouse at Ardoise, Nova Scotia, and devotes his time to researching and writing historical novels or anything else someone will pay him to write. His definition of "versatile" is "any gig in a storm." He's published eleven novels and CBC Radio has produced more than forty of his scripts.

Other Books by Alfred Silver

Lord of the Plains

Red River Story

Where the Ghost Horse Runs

Keepers of the Dawn

The Haunting of Maddie Prue

Three Hills Home: A Historical Novel of Acadians in Exile

Acadia, a novel

Clean Sweep

What the Critics Say

"Pungent characterizations and settings distinguish Silver's engrossing fiction."
– *Publishers Weekly*

"(Silver) knows how to entertain, how to spin a yarn and how to bring characters to life . . ." – *Lethbridge Herald*

Acadia – "A rollicking read about the escapades of those larger-than-life characters who dominated the early days of European thirst for dominance in the New World." – *Atlantic Books Today*

Lord of the Plains – "Abiding and earthy humour . . . a big, blustery, and satisfying piece of historical fiction." – *Kirkus Reviews*

Where the Ghost Horse Runs – "Finely crafted . . . Has the grandeur and grace of endlessly rolling tall-grass prairie." – *Winnipeg Free Press*

Keepers of the Dawn – "It's about time someone wrote an eminently readable novel about an Indian woman leader, and Alfred Silver has done it in superb fashion with Molly Brant . . . Wonderfully entertaining." – Allan W. Eckert, author of *The Frontiersman*

The Haunting of Maddie Prue – "[A] most mysterious, mystical and unconventional work of fiction." – *Winnipeg Free Press*

". . . I found it highly readable, with great characters and a good crime plot."
– Margaret Cannon, Crime Picks, *The Globe and Mail*